MA

# Manual

DAREN KING

**ff**

*faber and faber*

First published in 2008
by Faber and Faber Limited
3 Queen Square London WC1N 3AU

Typeset by Faber and Faber Ltd
Printed and bound in the UK by CPI Mackays, Chatham ME5 8TD

A CIP record for this book
is available from the British Library

ISBN 978-0-571-23066-2

2 4 6 8 10 9 7 5 3 1

# MANUAL

The sky is pink
The clouds are blue
In Patsy's world
Everything is true

'All around us were dogs. There were dogs talking and walking and flying. Dogs were howling round us in the wind. Dogs were lifting up. We had to keep from barking.'

Patsy

# I

I tell Patsy to keep away from the dogs. She looks confused, so I take her hand and lead her across the lawn.

The grass is long, but dry. It has been a long, dry summer. The wind today is the arrival of autumn. Tomorrow, leaves will dance on the grass.

Patsy is built like a carthorse. This is how Patsy describes herself.

Patsy is from a posh family. Patsy is well-to-do.

'I'm sorry about the dogs. My son is coming to walk them. Don't worry, he won't come into the house.'

There's a stone birdbath here, which, according to Patsy, contains owl food.

I ask the client what he does for a living.

'I'm a doctor, a GP.'

This is the dining table, where the client eats his breakfast, reads *The Times*, opens the post.

We sit and drink tea.

Through the glass, we see the gate open, the son fasten leads round the dogs' necks.

Patsy asks, 'What sort of animal is that? They look like brown paper bags.'

This is Patsy's cowgirl outfit. Denim shirt, can-can dress.

Black boots like old-fashioned kettles.

'I thought you'd be dressed differently. On your website you wear fetish gear.'

The website is an advert. It, I explain, is not real.

The client tells Patsy how he likes to be beaten, the severity. He fetches a paddle, a gag, string. He likes to be tied into a chair and left. Here, by the glass door.

I ask about the dogs, the son. He will see you through the glass.

I instruct the client to strip to his underpants and stand, while Patsy and I make comments in rhyme. This is an idea Patsy had during the first session. We focus on his hair, his physique. Your hair so fair, your back so slack.

I bend the client over the table, tie him to the tabletop. Here, by the glass door.

We sit on the patio and read *The Times*.

# 2

The client wants to meet in a café, to discuss. This is unusual. This will cost extra. The client is young, mid-twenties. His skin is dark. The client is sitting at a table. The client looks at the Coke can, the glass.

Patsy tells me that the client is an Indian prince. She wants to sniff his hair.

Patsy has the most beautiful eyes I have ever seen.

The waitress asks if we want anything.

No. We do not.

The client hands me money. I stand by the table and count. Patsy waits by the counter, arms folded behind her back, folded on the fake wood.

The client is bilingual, multilingual, and yet he cannot tell us what he wants.

'What would you do to me,' the client says, 'if I said you could do anything you chose?'

What would we do?

Nothing. We would do nothing.

Patsy steps up to the table, whispers into the client's ear. The client smiles, confused. Later, I ask Patsy what she told him. 'What did you tell him, what did you say?'

But Patsy does not know.

The client moves his fingers on the Coke can, talks. 'I'm getting married. I want to do something I have never done before.'

Outside, clouds roll, gathering grey.

The client looks at the table.

The door opens, a line of glass sweeping the floor. A girl walks in. Almond eyes, ruby bracelet, sandals.

Cars stop, start.

The client sits up, hand moves from the Coke. Looks at me. His face tells me to walk away. The girl saw him from outside, was walking past, on her way somewhere, or home from somewhere, from work. Here is her boy, her fiancé, her Indian prince. Here, in this café, with this man, and the girl with boots made of tin.

'You said you wouldn't do it,' the girl says.

'I'm not going to do it. I told him I don't want to do it.'

In my hand, money.

'You've paid him. Why pay him if you're not going to do it?'

The client and the girl walk out.

His hair, Patsy tells me, smelt of gunpowder.

# 3

The client takes the key from his trouser pocket, his suit.

The wife is at work, thinks he is at work. He was. He sneaked back.

'How about we massage each other and we both get a happy ending?'

No. No happy ending.

We do not offer that service.

When we arrived, there was no client. Red front door, red doorstep. Suburban terrace. Trees shedding leaves, removing their clothes.

I waited with Patsy on the lawn.

When I step onto the drive, my trainers are wet.

The client tells us that the world of business is a series of levels, like in a computer game.

This man is not understood. He can speak at a conference, he can delegate. He can motivate a sales fleet of forty. Yet, he cannot get through to his wife.

'I didn't realise there would be two of you. Did you bring oil?'

I did not bring oil. I do not offer that service.

The client has oil. His wife is a massage therapist. She works on his lumbago. This is the only time his wife is permitted to touch him. Her room is the room across the landing, the room they intended for their child, the child they will never have. But they will stay together, they took a vow. The client is a man of his word. A deal's a deal.

This is not a deal.

The client hides the plastic bottle in his hand.

'We travelled across London,' I say in the bathroom. 'You have to pay us, for our time.'

Patsy hops across the tiles, a game, do not step on the cracks.

We could tie him up, rob him, leave. But, we cannot tie him up. The client did not request bondage. What he wants is a full body rubdown.

Patsy and the client have a conversation about self-defence. A trained nurse, Patsy knows how to protect herself.

The client twists to the floor, laughs, impressed.

Patsy sits on the client, astride his chest, the silk tie creased, a fold. 'Stop now.'

What if your wife comes home?

Is this her photograph, is this her face?

'My wife won't return for hours. Stop now.'

I tell Patsy that this is what he wants, that he is play acting, that he is a baby. What this client needs is a smack.

Patsy unbuckles the client's belt, tugs his pants and trousers to his knees, lifts the legs, a mother changing a nappy, slap.

The client is not pleased. He does not want this. He wants it to stop.

'You can't sit on me all day.'

I look at the clock.

Patsy bends the client's arm.

Patsy's bottom could sink a battleship.

I walk down to the kitchen, count to ten, clang something, walk back up.

'What did you do in the kitchen?'

'I wrote a note for your wife.'

I tell Patsy to help the client to his feet. He has something to find, on a different level.

On the stairs, the client unfolds his tie.

A car pulls into the drive.

'Where is it? Why are you doing this to me?'

'You have to pay.'

The client hands me money. I stand by the kitchen door, count.

'Where's the bloody note?'

There is no note. It is in your head.

The car was a neighbour, turning round.

Out in the street, we look at the photographs. The client and his wife. The client and his empty home. His childless marriage, without love, without sex. The scent of massage oil. Bergamot, jasmine, lavender, rose. Patsy put the bottles into her bag.

# 4

The client hit a burglar with a frying pan. Hit him so hard the handle broke. The boy had climbed in through the kitchen window. This window, by the client's head.

'There's nothing like a biscuit,' the client says, dunking the biscuit in his tea. 'Do you want cash or cheque?'

Cash, in full, at the start.

The client chased the boy down the street. Knocked him off his mountain bike. Twenty years old. The pan span through the air, clonk.

Patsy ties the client to the radiator.

I open the client's piggy bank. Pull the pink plug. Coins fall out. The coins make a lot of noise. 1p, 2p, 20p, 10p, 1p. On the shelf, on the floor.

Patsy tickles the client's belly with a feather.

I look inside the fridge. Orange juice, from concentrate. Tin of corned beef, open, the metal lid curled, bent. Three cans of Coke.

The client is bound, gagged.

A fat, pink pig.

We use the client's duvet cover as a picnic blanket. This is unhygienic. What do you get up to in bed? Do you leave the light on? Do you keep your socks on?

This is the client's list. Bondage, humiliation, verbal.

The client called the police as he ran. Yelled into his mobile phone. Held the boy in front of a CCTV camera until the police arrived.

We spread the tea things on the blanket. Corned beef sandwiches with the crusts cut off. Ice cream, jelly. Orange squash. On the cups, pictures of teddy bears at a picnic, like this picnic, but fun.

The client is tied to the washing machine. Patsy tapes a teddy bear to the client's back.

Patsy finds a corkscrew in the cutlery drawer. A tail for the fat, pink pig. We do not proceed, for legal reasons.

In the client's study, a 5-megapixel digital camera. We smear jam on the client's bottom and take photographs.

The client has a desk, a PC. The client has a photoprinter. There are options.

We print passport-size photographs, cut them out, hide them around the house. We do not know why we do this.

# 5

The pub is in North London, Tottenham. The client sneaked us in round the back, up the fire escape.

In the kitchen, flowers. Patsy picks through the flowers, stabs the stems into her hair. This while the client eats.

This is the client's lounge. Bay window, net curtains, wall unit, television.

The kitchen smells of brown sauce.

I tell Patsy that she is a dancer, and she dances, nearly breaks a vase, pirouettes, stubs her big toe.

Do not tell Patsy things.

Downstairs, behind the bar, the wife serves drinks.

The client closes the window, fastens the metal frame, swallows the last bit of sausage roll.

The client takes off jeans, shirt, socks. Flings his underpants at a painting.

Patsy ties the client's hands, ties the rope to the banister.

Your belly like jelly, your feet so neat.

We look at the CDs. The client has opera for lovers, the best of the seventies, the eighties, the nineties. Music to drive to, music to do the washing up.

'We need a sock,' Patsy says, 'for his mouth.' She sorts through the drawer, finds a sock.

Then, voices.

We walk to the bottom of the stairs. We listen.

From the bar, voices.

A door opens, opened by a woman. The woman is confused, angry. 'Who the hell are you?'

We're with your husband. Upstairs.

'Upstairs? I live on my own.'

Patsy kicks the front door.

Patsy opens the front door.

In my pocket, the money, a sausage roll.

# 6

The client has his head in his hands.

Through the window, on the driveway, the client's car. The client's car is a Jag.

We sit with the client on the sofa, the creaky leather.

The client's wife is dead. She was murdered, strangled. 'Her death has been the most devastating event of my life,' the client tells us. 'I cry often, uncontrollably.'

On the table, a newspaper. The world of broadcasting becomes increasingly complicated to navigate, it says here. We turn away. We switch off.

The client tells us that she will never be. 'She will never be.' Never be what?

He sobs. Sobbing.

The client wants to be beaten. He wants to feel pain that is not mental, not emotional. Pain that is not inside.

Patsy removes the client's trousers, pants. Socks remain on. The socks are red. Not the socks of a man in mourning, Patsy says. This whispered into my ear.

I tie the client to the coffee table.

The client stops crying. He is switched off.

Patsy smacks the client's bottom with a squash racket.

The client owns a permanent marker. It can write on

anything, anything but itself. Remove the cap, write it down. We write words, phrases on the client's skin. Left, right, on his bottom. I need my inhaler, across his back. My wife is dead.

The client will read these words, in mirror writing. The client will scrub the words with salt.

The client has an office, a study. He has a briefcase, a filing cabinet, an oak desk. The client has a cleaner. Monday, Thursday. Today is Thursday. The cleaner starts at five, while the client is at squash.

Today, the client will not play squash.

I tell Patsy to untie the client.

'He will see the words,' Patsy tells me, 'reflected in your shimmering gaze.'

In Patsy's world, everything is true.

We lie on the client's bed, hold hands. The cleaner will let herself in. She will find the client, scream, walk out. Unsure, the cleaner will stand in the road. We will hear the key turn in the lock. This, from up here, on the client's bed.

We take the plastic boxes from Patsy's bag and eat the packed lunch. Sandwiches with the crusts cut off.

At ten to five, we let ourselves out.

# 7

Not all emails are genuine. There are timewasters, hoaxers. There are clients who do not know what they want.

A couple would like to hire our bedroom, our bed. Patsy thunders down the hall, to ask Owl.

Owl is not amused. Turns his head 360 degrees, in that way of his. Through the window, button eyes spy a vole.

Owl lives on that bed. The pillow is his nest, his home. A bird needs a place to ponder. Owl is an intellectual, a thinker.

There are people who make porn movies. They require someone to use, abuse. Someone to hold the camera.

No, we do not offer that service.

We receive an email from a journalist. I am writing an article on domination, fetish. Can we talk?

If you pay for my time, yes.

We meet in a scruffy pub in Bethnal Green, down the road from the flat. Pasty waits in the wings, with Owl. The journalist buys me a pint of lager. Her eyebrows are black, the fringe blonde. She asks questions, notebook open, pen poised.

What sort of people are your clients?

Well, what sort of people?

Are they all male?

I do not know, have nothing to say.

Patsy on a wooden stool at the back, rocking, lifting the legs. Owl perched on the top of the cigarette machine, watching pensively. Falls off when change clatters.

'There is a lot I could tell you, but I am unable to do so for legal reasons.'

What legal reasons? Michael?

'I am unable to discuss that for legal reasons.'

Has something happened? Did a session get out of hand? Are you being taken to court?

'I am very anxious to clear my name.'

In my hand, phrases cut from a newspaper.

The journalist stands, walks out.

Patsy dances across the pub, tugs a man's belt loop, drinks the journalist's drink. We brush dust from Owl's tummy feathers, laugh.

'Owl takes things too seriously,' Pasty says.

'Owl is a night bird. Lots of young voles come out of their nests for supper. And kittens too.'

Patsy

# 8

Someone has been in our flat. Things have moved around. Not theft, everything is here.

The speakers, the sides that look like wood but are not wood, are here. The three circles that move, vibrate.

The television, not plugged in, no face.

Owl, Patsy, me.

Outside, shiny brown leaves sparkle, reflect the bright autumn sun.

Here is the bed, its squeak that Owl mistakes for a mouse, and swoops down to eat when Patsy throws him.

Here, the amplifier Patsy poured wine into. Her hands wide apart. Patsy thought her hands were close together. In one hand the bottle, the other, the empty wine glass. The hot machine sizzled. I switched off the mains, unscrewed screws, the magnetic screwdriver holding them. Beneath the lid, a city, the end of the world, the buildings futuristic, the rivers blood red.

We dried the circuit board with tissue Patsy fetched from the bathroom.

Patsy is like me. She is someone who has experienced a lot of pain for no reason.

Here, Patsy's dressing-up box, her wooden trunk. Inside,

clothes mix together like paint. Not just clothes. Birthday cards, mirror, glitter. Anything that shines, sparkles, excites.

At the window, trees dance in the breeze.

Patsy says it was Owl who moved things. Flapped his wings and the room changed. Owl does not move things, I explain. Owl is tired. Owl has beak flu.

Patsy fetches paracetamol, mashed up with cake.

I read the business news. The growing international crisis, catastrophic oil price spike, crude oil at $100 a barrel. A single political shock could send the world market into panic.

'At least we have our health,' Patsy says, 'unlike poor Owl.'

I explain to Patsy that it is not that simple. Analysts warn of a sharp rise in petrol prices. Empty forecourts, recession. If you can't afford petrol, you can't afford Patsy, me.

Patsy consults her owl book.

At the window, beyond the glass, trees hold hands.

Zero clients would mean zero income. No owl food or people food, no plastic bottles of supermarket wine. No home, no squeaky bed.

'Such business is not for owls,' Patsy says. She covers his tufty ears, cups the head with her palm.

Owl does not need to hear this. Owl thinks we work in telecoms.

Beyond the glass, trees turn red.

# 9

Owl gets frightened easily. He needs a cuddle, every now and then, to make him feel safe.

We arrived home last night to find that the dressing-up box had moved. It had been by the window. It was now in the centre of the room. On the bare boards, an oblong area without dust.

Patsy sorts through her dressing-up box, tossing clothes. I watch her dress. Skirt over skirt, petticoat over skirts. Upside down, inside out. Her make-up is two black lines, one below each eye.

I show Patsy a photograph of two dogs. The dogs look the same, are the same. The article explains that the dogs are sniffer dogs, trained to detect counterfeit DVDs. Their noses pick up the chemicals used in production. Piracy is linked to people trafficking, drugs.

Patsy says the dogs use their snouts.

Patsy has a self-destructive streak. I myself have a self-destructive streak. We are self-destructive. That is the worst thing to be because it means that you cannot become anything, you will only ever be yourself.

The dogs are not real dogs. The dogs are dogs in a photograph.

Owl was knitted by an old lady in a charity shop. Patsy designed Owl herself, on the back of an owl-coloured envelope. Paid the lady two pounds, gave her day meaning.

Our day does not have meaning.

Dogs have two hundred million sensitive cells in their nose, or snout. Dogs can taste smell, dogs do what they want. The dogs have not read the article. To dogs, the words have no meaning.

Through the window, office blocks shimmer, shine.

The old lady knitted Owl for two days, the wool dark as moss. She plumped him up, tried to give him shape. Stuffed him with white polyester stuffing. Button eyes gave him meaning.

Who moved the dressing-up box?

Owl could not have moved it. Owl is cushion sized.

Patsy can move the wooden trunk with one finger, one thumb. Patsy is as strong as a pit pony, her description. But it wasn't Patsy who moved the wooden trunk. When I closed the door, Patsy was standing in the road.

Owl was here, and Owl is wise.

Who was it, Owl?

Did you see them? Did you catch them?

# 10

I have a feeling of pain. I am coming down with something. The feeling is in my muscles or joints. I could take paracetamol but that will take the pain away and then I will have nothing, only Patsy, who I love dearly, and also Owl.

Patsy wipes my forehead with a pair of knickers.

The television is switched off. I do not allow Patsy to watch television.

No, Owl. You cannot watch a documentary about planets.

The knickers are clean, unworn. Patsy took the knickers from her wooden trunk. I listened as Patsy turned the tap. The water hit the sink, the knickers. Patsy held the knickers under the tap, pressed the knickers against my forehead.

Reflected in the blank television, the window, the sky.

I lie on the bed. Patsy helps with the legs.

Here are newspapers. Patsy bought the newspapers at the newsagent on Bethnal Green Road.

Patsy plumps up the pillows, Owl.

Patsy lifts my arm, tucks Owl under my arm.

Patsy, a trained nurse, kisses my forehead. Owl gets a kiss too, on the beak.

At the window, trees. The trees move.

Patsy checks the email. I instruct Patsy from the bed. Click, read.

There is an email from a businessman. His name is Edward. He wants to meet us. He has a proposition.

Patsy fetches a glass of tap water.

There is an email from a man in Brazil. The man replied to our ad. I will be in London on business, the man typed. Patsy tells me this. Patsy types her reply. I want to set up an owl sanctuary, Patsy types.

I read the business news.

Customer information could potentially have been accessed by unauthorised workers, I read.

Patsy wipes my forehead with the knickers. 'It's beak flu. You caught it from Owl.'

I cannot catch beak flu. I do not have a beak. I tell Patsy this.

'It mutated.'

Patsy replies to the email. I tell Patsy what to type. I have beak flu or nose flu. We will meet next week. We will meet when I am better.

Patsy consults Owl's medical book. There is a list of symptoms. Laughing while eating. Elongation of the face and hands.

I look at the room. This is here, that is over there. If things move, I will know.

Investment bank joins row over recruitment initiative.

At the window, trees hang their heads.

I close the curtains.

I instruct Patsy to tidy the top of the curtains. In boots like old-fashioned kettles, Patsy stands on the bed.

The bar is in Liverpool Street, the City of London.

Edward emailed from his work email account. I visited the company's website. On the website, information.

Through the window, Edward's office. The building is made of glass, steel. Blinds are pulled up, down. Behind the glass, figures.

The bar is modern. Square stools, square lights.

The bar is called Box.

There are men in suits. I have never worn a suit. I wear trainers, jeans.

At the scrubbed wood table, Patsy sings.

I look at the clock. The clock is above the bar. On the clock, information.

We wait for Edward.

A girl kicks off her shoes. Pointy shoes, pink as feet. The girl drops her shoes onto the scrubbed wood floor.

The door opens. A man walks in. The man wears a suit, shoes. In his hand, a red sheet of paper. This is a signal, a sign.

Patsy waves.

The man is Edward. The man removes his jacket. Edward fixes his cufflinks. Hairy hands, gold watch, leather strap.

Edward in his bespoke pinstripe suit.

Edward works in finance, futures. What are futures? Do we have a future, Edward? Patsy and me? How long can this go on?

'A futures contract is a standardised contract to purchase or sell standard commodities at a pre-set price,' Edward says.

At the bar, girls. The girls drink cocktails, wine. Mouths open when they laugh.

'We should not have met here,' Edward says. 'My colleagues drink here.'

'We are your colleagues,' I say.

Edward thinks that this is a joke. It is not a joke.

'Shall we get a cab?'

Out in the street, Edward stops a taxi.

Above, buildings, sky. I look up at the sky.

Inside the taxi, we do not speak. I look out of the window. Liverpool Street, Marble Arch, Paddington. The driver does not speak. I would not listen.

The taxi stops outside a hotel. The building is white. There are pillars.

Edward pays the driver.

On the pavement, we watch the taxi pull away from the kerb.

In Edward's pocket, a key. Edward takes the key from his pocket. The key is attached to a plastic fob. On the plastic fob, a number, 11.

Edward opens the glass door.

We follow Edward into the hotel. There is a man here. The man is sitting behind the desk. Edward waves the key at the man.

We follow Edward up the stairs, along the corridor, to a door. On the door, a number, 11.

Edward opens the door. We follow Edward through the door.

There is a girl here.

Edward kisses the girl on the cheek. 'This is Baby Girl,' Edward says. 'I call her that. I want you to call her that, too. Baby, meet Michael and Patsy.'

'My real name is Rebecca.'

Baby Girl is young, pretty. Pink blouse, skirt, no shoes. The tights are silver.

Patsy asks Baby Girl her age.

'Eighteen. Why?'

Patsy scowls. Patsy is thirty. I am thirty. Edward is fifty, fifty-five.

Edward paces the carpet, fixes his cufflinks, frowns. 'We're not going to do this today,' Edward says.

'I thought we were,' Baby Girl says. 'I do feel ready.'

Edward looks at Patsy, me. 'We need to know each other better.'

Edward wants us to leave.

In the street, I open the envelope, count.

# 12

I pull my sweatshirt over my head, drop it onto the floor.

Patsy has bought drinks. I instructed her to do this. Lager for me, wine for Patsy, vole-blood cola for Owl.

I sit with Patsy on the squishy sofa.

Opposite, three girls. The girls have jobs, a career. The three are colleagues. I hear them discuss work, boyfriends. What he said, what he did. And what I really love is the way he says things.

I turn pages.

The girls are friends. I do not have friends. I have Patsy, Owl. Patsy does not need friends, does not live in that world.

Patsy thinks that I am gorgeous. I think that Patsy is beautiful. Mary Poppins with a big bottom.

I drop the book onto the table.

The girls do not know me. I am unknown. I am an unknown quantity. I am no quantity, am in fact nothing. I play no part in this world. From outside, I look in. Any glass I peer through is one way.

The girls work in the media. I work in the media, too. I will tell them this.

On the table, the owl book, fanning open.

Patsy takes Owl from her bag, sits him between us, his woolly feathers warming the leather.

The girls eat something green. Stuffed vine leaves, the girl said. You cannot buy crisps here.

The girls look at Owl.

What is that? That there? That thing there?

This? This is Owl.

I hold Owl, lift him up. Owl swoops over the table, hovers, flapping his clever wings.

Owl has a way of breaking the ice. Owl is not shy. For an intellectual, Owl is very sociable.

'He's for work,' I say. 'Part of a project.'

'What project? What do you do?'

I tell the girls that we work in advertising. This is Patricia Reaner, my PA.

There is music. A female vocalist sings about the blues. I have got the blues, she sings. I ain't got this, I ain't got that. I have got the blues.

I have not got the blues. I have got Patsy, Owl.

'Why have you brought it to a bar?' asks one of the girls.

Patsy scowls. It?

Owl screeches. Control yourself, Owl. Think of a vole, any vole.

The girls talk, discuss. There is never time to do things, to get things done.

I do not get things done. I do not have things to get done.

Outside, a car alarm.

Owl's ears prick up. A robot vole?

'You excite me, I find you gorgeous, skin like a white milk orchid and hair blacker than the night.'

Patsy

# 13

I read the business pages. I read, but I do not understand. The equity bull market is dead, I read. This, according to City experts.

At my table, a girl touches a girl's wrist. The girl has something to say.

I wait, read, fail to understand.

At the flat, I kissed Patsy goodbye, said goodbye.

The pages are numbered and lettered. B2, B3.

Analysts fear sharp correction around the world. The market is due a correction. To Edward and me, correction means two different things.

Men remove their ties, fold their arms. I cannot do this. I do not own a tie. I wear trainers, jeans. I can fold my arms. I do this.

Square stools, square lamps.

At the scrubbed wood table, I wait.

Men talk business. 'We don't want to take a macro risk,' one says. They discuss girls. They discuss money.

I earn more per hour than some lawyers. Yet, I am worth less.

Through the window, across the street, Edward's office.

Then, through the door, Edward. I watch Edward walk

through the door. The door swings closed behind Edward. I watch Edward approach the bar, buy a drink. The drink is whisky or a drink that looks like whisky. There is ice. Edward turns. Edward walks towards me. Edward walks past me.

I am not Edward's colleague. My colleagues are Patsy, Owl.

Here are Edward's colleagues. The men shake Edward's hand. The women kiss him. This is Colleen, Jude. This is Topaz. This is Robert, Ian, James.

The women have jobs, a career.

Edward looks at me. Ah, Michael. Edward touches the arm of a girl. The girl turns, looks at me.

Owl, swoop in.

But Owl is not here.

Edward and the girl cross the bar. At my table, Edward frowns. Edward is not pleased. 'Why are you here? Did we arrange to meet?'

No. We did not.

'Then why are you here?'

I am reading the newspaper. I tell Edward this.

Edward touches the newspaper. 'You're reading the business section. If my colleagues find out how we met, Michael, it would be embarrassing to say the least. You do know that I'm married.'

I did not know this.

The girl smiles. The girl is Baby.

'I did mean to contact you. I still intend to hire you.'

'We're going to a party,' Baby Girl says.

'Tomorrow,' Edward says.

'I thought the party was today.'

In Edward's hand, a sheet of paper. On the sheet of paper, a list of names. Who are these people, Edward? Who is in your world?

'Can we take Michael to the party?'

'No,' Edward says. 'My wife will be there.'

'That's why we should take him,' Baby Girl says.

Edward adjusts cufflinks. 'Ah.'

# 14

I had not seen Adrian since school. I recognised Adrian in the street. I told Adrian about the flat, that someone goes in, that objects are moved.

In the plastic carrier bag, a webcam, cables.

Adrian works in computers.

Adrian studies films. The history of cinema.

'Do you know how many films are cut these days? Three per cent. Three decades ago it was thirty.'

Who was in our flat? Who moved things?

I sit on the bed with Owl. Like me, Owl has no value, no meaning.

'It used to be about decency. Now they only censor when the film encourages you to break the law.'

In Adrian's hand, the webcam.

'What do you do, Michael?'

I tell Adrian that I look after a girl.

'You're a pimp?'

No.

'Then what are you?'

I don't know.

But Adrian does know. 'You work in the fetish industry. I ran into Kenneth from school. He said he hired you for a session.'

I had not recognised Kenneth. Naked, tied to the garden fence, a pillow case over his head, Kenneth looked different.

Adrian has tablets. I do not ask.

Owl thinks the tablets are sweets. Don't eat the red ones, Owl.

Adrian counts the tablets into his hand. Red, cream and white, dark blue. With numbers, letters.

Adrian drops one of the tablets.

In the kitchen, I turn the tap. I hold the glass under the cold tap.

'I can't believe you haven't got any cutlery.'

We have chopsticks, plastic chip forks, cocktail sticks.

In the bedroom, the computer screen, my face.

# 15

Edward puts his hands on our shoulders. 'Two friends of mine, Michael and Rebecca.'

The house is in Maida Vale. The house is large. Balcony, roof-top terrace. This window is round.

In the garden, trees. In the trees, leaves, lights. The lights are white, bright.

The front door opens. The woman stands, smiles. The woman is the woman who opened the door. Slender fingers stroke the stem. The woman drinks wine from a wine glass.

You're together, Edward said. This, to me. I am hiring you to escort Baby Girl, so that she can attend the party.

The woman leads us into the house.

'Is my wife here?'

'Alicia? She isn't. I thought you'd be coming together.'

Edward looks at me, shrugs.

The woman takes our coats, Edward's umbrella.

'This jumper started out blue,' a man says. 'I washed it and it turned a queasy purple.'

I ask Edward if he wants me to leave.

'No. Alicia will have friends here. Stay.'

We walk into the lounge. Come through to the lounge.

There is no music. There are voices, there is the sound of

a machine. I do not look at the machine. The machine is art. The man tells me this.

A woman in a suit asks me if I had a productive day.

I nod.

'What do you do?'

'I work in an office, like you.'

'But what do you do?'

I tell the woman that I work with computers.

'What area? Systems? Networks?'

'Email.'

The woman raises an eyebrow.

A man laughs.

Baby Girl holds my hand.

In black and white, the man holds a tray.

Baby takes two drinks from the tray. The colour of the wine is red. The colour is the colour of blood, berries, your lips.

A man asks who I am with.

'Baby Girl,' I say. I touch Baby's arm.

'He calls me Baby because of the picture on my T-shirt,' Baby Girl says. 'I'm Rebecca.'

I look at Baby's T-shirt. Lace, buttons. There is not a picture of a baby.

The man looks at the T-shirt.

'I'm not wearing it today,' Baby says. Baby punches me. This, on the arm, here.

Through the door, the balcony. On the balcony, people.

The dining table is for coke. Baby Girl tells me this. The tabletop is glass. People stand at the table.

A man rolls a fifty-pound note into a tube.

Baby Girl has coke. She takes the envelope from her bag.

On the shelf, books. The shelf is a bookshelf. Owl would be in his element.

A woman flicks through a book.

Books are worthless, like me, Patsy, our life together, our lives.

Baby tells me she steals things. What things? I ask Baby Girl to explain.

'Nothing valuable. Me and my friend stole a toilet seat. We had to rip it off. It made a horrible sound.'

A man asks Baby if the toilet seat was clean.

'Of course. Who wants a dirty toilet seat?'

More coke. A man asks if he can have some. He can. The man puts the tube to his nose. The tube is a ten-pound note. The tube is orange, brown.

Baby Girl touches my leg, the denim. 'Do you want coke?'

'No.'

The tabletop is a mirror. The lighting creates the effect. There are two lines. I can see my face. I look like an invader.

A woman throws a sandwich over the balcony.

Edward is here. Edward holds Baby Girl.

Baby looks at me, laughs.

A man asks me how I know Edward. I tell the man that I am Edward's employee. The statement is false.

The man talks about business, work.

I make a comment. The man laughs. The man thinks that the comment was funny, that I am a funny person. Perhaps I am a funny person without value.

Women chink glasses. No other objects make this sound.

I am worried about Patsy.

Baby Girl asks me if I want to see her period.

46

Baby takes my hand, leads me between people, up the stairs, to a room. The room is a bedroom. One man walks out of the bedroom. The man winks. The bedroom is empty.

Baby sits on the bed.

On the bed, coats.

I watch Baby roll down her tights. The tights are black, opaque. Short skirt, strappy shoes. The buckles are tiny.

On Baby's thigh, a cut. Baby has been hurt. There is blood. Baby pinches the skin. 'It looks like a vagina,' Baby Girl says.

I look at the wall.

I walk out of the room.

I walk down the stairs, down the hall, out of the house, into the street.

In the street, I find Patsy.

'I was attacked by a drunken banshee,' Patsy says. 'She called me a whore and said my socks didn't go with my shoes. Owl had to fly to the police.'

# 16

At the table, we wait.

I want to talk about your work, Edward said on the telephone. It's an exciting world, from the outside.

The café is in Holborn, Chancery Lane. Through the window, the street, trees, shops.

I hold Patsy's hand. This between pepper and salt.

Baby wants to work in the fetish industry. Edward told me this on the telephone. I do not believe this.

The café is called Sarahs. There is no apostrophe. The café does not belong to Sarah. The café contains Sarahs, plural.

Patsy does not want to teach Baby Girl. 'She weighs less than Owl. And Owl is light as a feather.'

Patsy is cross.

Patsy folds her arms.

'Clients will like that,' I explain. 'The smaller the dom, the more the client has to submit.'

A taxi stops outside the café. In the back of the taxi, Edward, Baby Girl. Edward kisses Baby Girl. Heads turn. The hand covers Baby's face.

Tree leaves shuffle, rearrange.

I look at the salt, pepper, ketchup, brown sauce.

Edward and Baby climb out of the taxi. The taxi door slams closed. I hear this.

Wind blows hair across Edward's face. The hair is Baby Girl's hair. Baby Girl has long hair. If I walked beside Baby, the hair would touch my face.

Behind me, at the counter, a man orders pie and chips. No, mash. Changed my mind, the man says.

Baby's palm flat against the glass. The hand pushes the door.

Baby Girl walks across the tiles. Bare legs, strappy shoes. Toenails painted tongue pink.

Baby kisses my cheek, shakes Patsy's hand.

'You're minuscule,' Patsy says. 'I could snap you like a twig.'

Baby does not like this.

'It's starting to rain,' Edward says.

Baby Girl and Edward sit at our table. Orange plastic seats. The pattern on the table is brown-orange check.

I tell Baby Girl how it works. I tell her about the website, the emails. Enquiries, queries, questions. Booking details. I tell her about timewasters, no-shows.

'But what about the work?'

'You tie them up and spank them.'

'What if they ask for something weird? They want you to kill them or something?'

At the window, rain, needles.

Patsy orders drinks. Lager for Edward, me. For Baby Girl, Coke. For Patsy, nothing. Owl is not present.

The woman puts the bottles on the counter.

Patsy carries the bottles from the counter. The bottles are ice cold. Condensation loosens the labels. Hold the bottle, slide the label with your hand.

The woman brings glasses. The woman pours the drinks.

'If you peel the label it means you're sexually frustrated,' Baby Girl says.

Patsy peels the label.

Patsy makes Baby Girl nervous. She tends to do that.

In the street, people pull up their collars. There are husbands, there are wives. High heels arch over puddles. Men step over puddles.

The door open, closed.

In Baby's cardigan pocket, a plastic toy dog. Baby Girl puts the dog on the table.

I ask Baby the dog's name.

'Yelper.'

Patsy looks at me, at the dog on the table, at Baby's pink hand.

'I had a dream where I had a pet dog this big,' Baby Girl says. 'I asked the pet shop if they had a tiny dog and they said you couldn't get them. Edward bought me this.'

The window looks like it is coated in polythene.

Patsy lifts her bag onto the table. The bag is a sports bag. Purple, leather. Inside the bag, Patsy's toy farm. Busy hands set up the farm on the table. Cute and fun-looking farm animals, it says on the box.

Rain slaps the glass.

The farm was made by a company called Bully Build. Patsy says that this is the best name for a toy-farm manufacturer she has ever heard.

Baby helps Patsy position the animals.

Four cows, one calf.

Two pink pigs.

A horse.

These made of wood. Moveable head, legs.

The sheep has a woolly coat, stuck on with glue.

'I like my dog best,' Baby Girl says. 'It's like the dog in my dream.'

Patsy has dreams too.

Patsy takes Baby Girl's dog and runs out into the street.

Chairs move.

On the table, the empty Coke bottle, bottles of beer. Cows, pigs, sheep, horse. The wooden box.

On the floor, Patsy's upturned bag.

I walk out into the street.

Baby Girl remains inside, with Edward. It is warm there.

Patsy stopping traffic. Runs across the road. Black boots step into puddles. Weave between taxis, a police car. Patsy, me. On the pavement, I put my arms around Patsy's waist.

Patsy is like Owl. She needs a cuddle, every now and then, to make her feel safe.

# 17

Baby wants to sit upstairs, at the back. You can slump, Baby says. You can lollop like a tongue.

Patsy frowns. 'That's no way to talk.'

At the café, Patsy dropped the dog onto the table.

At the café, Edward said goodbye. Take Baby Girl with you. Teach her. Show her the ropes.

Holborn, Liverpool Street. The flat is in Bethnal Green.

On Patsy's lap, Patsy's bag. The bag is open. Farm animals stare at the bus ceiling.

Bully Build. Cute and fun-looking farm animals.

'You can get a barn,' Patsy says. 'The roof is made of rubber.'

Voices, engine, traffic.

The windscreen wiper squeaks. A stretched black mouse.

'When Edward pays us, you can buy the whole farm.'

Patsy squeezes my hand.

We found the flat three years ago in *Loot*. I wrote the address in the margin. Remove the cap, write it down. Patsy leant forward, her back a sturdy oak table.

Patsy wants to throw Baby's toy dog out of the window. Do not do this. Yelper learns to fly. Owl would laugh if you told him.

On the back seat, Baby Girl stretched out. Shoes lost in floor dust. Bare feet press against the glass, the condensation. Toes wriggle at faces. Another bus alongside.

Two men get on. The men climb the stairs. Black faces, hooded tops, trainers. The men want the back seat.

On Patsy's knee, sheep graze.

Baby wants to move forward, sit with us, but the men won't let her.

Rain taps the glass.

'You going somewhere, baby?'

'Don't make that face, baby.'

It's like they know her name.

Black hands on pink thighs. In the corner of Baby's mouth, a tongue, bus red.

Patsy looks at the men. In her head, thoughts. Chemicals whirl. Adrenalin, Prozac. Patsy puts the bag on my lap. Hold the farm, Michael, I'm going in.

'Don't make that face, baby.'

Patsy stomps down the swaying bus. Hands on hips. Swears, shouts.

The men try to squeeze past Patsy, but Patsy blocks them. Patsy has things to say.

Baby Girl sucks her thumb.

At the next stop, Baby gets off.

'I am a silly old woman who spent all her money on whatnots.'

Patsy

# 18

While Patsy is downstairs clanging about, I do forty sit-ups. If I hear clogs on the stairs, I will stop. I do not want to be laughed at, ever.

Owl turns away.

It is important, we are told. You have to look after yourself.

We got home yesterday to find the kitchen window broken. Broken glass on the grass, the windowsill, the pavement. Broken glass in the air when Patsy moved her hand. Blood on Patsy's hand.

I unlocked the front door, hid behind Patsy.

On the stairs, Patsy said that she was afraid. Upstairs, in the bathroom, Patsy said that she was frightened.

Who is in the bedroom? Have they gone? Did they move things?

No. They have taken things.

The television is not here. The speakers are not here. The amplifier Patsy poured wine into is not here.

There is the bed, the wardrobe, cupboards.

The computer is not here. Adrian's webcam is not here. No carrier bag, no cables.

Where is Owl?

Ah, Owl is here. Owl has not been taken.

Or, he was taken. Owl flew back.

Patsy's dressing-up box is not here. No clothes, no shoes.

Who did this, Owl? Who has been in our flat? Who has taken things?

The seven iPods are not here. Stolen from clients, stolen from us.

Whoever did this had a key. The front door was locked. The dressing-up box would not fit through the kitchen window, and the dressing-up box has gone.

I ask Patsy about the landlord. Did he come round?

'Yes,' Patsy says. 'He said the cheque bounced. We have to move out.'

You did not tell me this.

'I told Owl to tell you. He said he'd send you a pecks message.'

Message not received.

Patsy scowls at Owl. 'You feathery little shit.'

My bank account is closed. This, due to bankruptcy. We pay the cash into Patsy's account. Miss Patricia J Reaner. We write the landlord a cheque. Remove the cap, write it down. Patsy signs the cheque.

In the kitchen, no cutlery. The cutlery was not taken. We do not own cutlery.

Patsy packs her bag. There is not much to pack. Food, Owl.

Outside, we step over flowers.

'I gave our money to an owl sanctuary,' Patsy says.

# 19

Alicia's Rooms is owned by Edward's wife. Edward invested in the business. Baby tells me this near the coats.

Patsy returns from the toilet. The purple leather sports bag swings between her legs.

Inside the bag, Owl.

'I can come here,' Baby Girl tells me. 'Alicia thinks I'm Edward's niece.'

'What if she finds out?'

'She won't find out. Edward's family are dead.'

The waiter shows us the table, where Edward faces the wall. He looks up, stands.

I turn away.

The lampshades are blue-white, the shape of mints.

Baby Girl sits with Edward. Patsy and I sit opposite. Behind Edward's head, the window, office buildings, St Paul's.

The waiter pours red wine.

'I will have my usual,' Edward tells the waiter. 'Whatever these are having.' Moves his hand. Turns the menu against the wood.

Baby wants pizza.

Owl wants vole. Patsy will drop it into her bag.

'Pinstripes make my eyes go funny,' Baby Girl tells me. I turn, follow Baby's gaze. Three men in suits discuss resources, strategy. In the street, they would pass me, not see me. Even here they do not see me.

Patsy tells Edward that we have no money.

'I know that,' Edward says. 'That's why I invited you here. To discuss.'

The waiter brings olives.

I tell Edward that we cannot pay for the meal.

'I thought you were earning good money. Why do you think I hired you to teach Baby to be a dominatrix? You earn two hundred pounds an hour. That's more than I pay my solicitor.'

'The two hundred is between us,' I explain, 'and that's when we can get the work.'

Edward scratches his chin. Edward has not shaved. 'How many sessions do you do in a week, Michael?'

'It varies.'

'On a good week?'

'One. Two.'

'A bad week?'

'None.'

Edward looks at the olives. Purple eyes stare back. Edward eats one, pops it into his mouth.

The sky darkens.

'But you have regular clients?'

'We did not do our job properly.'

'We lark about,' Patsy says.

'In what way? Michael?'

'We abuse the situation.'

'Yes, in what way?'

In the corner, a girl sweeps yellow petals. The petals look like sun rays, dried up and dropped off.

'I find the work boring.'

'All work is boring, Michael.'

No. All work is not boring. Your work is not boring.

Patsy tells Edward about the iPods. 'He had seven.'

'You stole them from clients?'

I nod.

'Well this is why you don't get repeat bookings. You can't fuck these people around and expect them to rehire you.'

Edward and Baby hold hands, talk.

I do not talk.

Patsy does not talk.

Inside Patsy's bag, Owl does not squawk.

The waiter brings Edward's meal, our bolognaise, Baby's pizza. 'My dad used to cut it.'

'I am not your father, Baby. We've established that.'

'You remind me of him.'

'Do I kiss like your father?'

Baby Girl shakes her head.

'Did he touch you the way I touch you?'

Baby laughs. Opens her mouth.

I look out of the window.

Edward cuts Baby's pizza in half, in half again.

On Edward's plate, meat. Edward slices the meat. Bites, chews, lowers his fork. 'I will take care of you, Michael. I have a flat you can use. But I want you to do something for me.'

In the street, a bus hides behind a tree.

'You offer a service. I may ask you to perform that service.'

'Which service exactly?'
Edward does not speak, eats.
In Patsy's lap, Owl pecks scraps.

## 20

Edward takes us to the flat. Do you always travel by taxi, Edward? In Edward's hand, keys. Edward unlocks the door, wipes his shoes on the mat.

'I'm not here often,' Edward says.

Patsy says that the flat is minute. Do not look a gift horse in the mouth, Patsy. We have no possessions, no home.

'The idea was to let to a young professional,' Edward says. 'Spacious studio in the City. But then I met Baby.'

I look at Baby Girl. Bare knees, white socks.

Behind Baby, Patsy slams the front door.

'It needs redecorating,' Edward says. 'The skirting boards have been painted.'

The carpet is snooker-table green.

The carpet is dusty. White paint where it meets the wood.

No curtains.

No lampshades.

No doors, only the front door. Doorways lead to bathroom, lounge.

Double bed, kitchen sink, fitted cupboards, microwave, cooker.

Edward sits on the mattress. 'Patsy, pop to the supermarket. I will draw you a map. Here's a list.' Edward opens his briefcase. Pad, pen. Remove the cap, write it down. Rips the page from the spiral, hands it to Patsy.

Biscuits, bread, milk, tea.

Toilet tissue, shower gel, soap.

Sandwich ham.

'I know the way,' Baby Girl says, and leads Patsy down the hall to the street.

I open the window. The Thames. Across the water, the Tower of London.

'Sit.'

I sit with Edward on the mattress.

'I need you to be strong for me, Michael, because I need you to look after Baby Girl. Do you think you can do that?'

I nod.

'Baby Girl self-harms. Do you know what that is?'

Yes.

'Does Patsy self-harm?'

No.

'A lot of girls do.'

Patsy is not a girl. Patsy is a woman. Patsy could snap you like a twig.

'I can't watch Baby day and night, Michael. That's why I'm letting you stay here. I have a leaflet.'

Edward reaches into his inside pocket.

I take the leaflet.

I laugh. This is an inappropriate response.

Understanding Self-Harm. A key information resource for young people who self-harm, their families and friends.

There are photographs. A boy in shadow, a girl in a darkened room.

Baby Girl is not the girl in the photograph.

Physical and psychological management. Secondary prevention. Primary and secondary care.

'Read it through, let me know what you think. I need to know that I can trust you. Do you have care experience, Michael?'

I care for Patsy, Owl.

I tell Edward that Patsy is schizophrenic. I do not know if this is true. To me, it is true. To Patsy, everything is true.

'I'm having a bathroom door put in,' Edward says, 'but no lock.'

Some people who self-harm commit suicide, it says here. Self-harm is the opposite of suicide. Self-harm is a way of coping with life. Suicide is giving up on life.

'I give Baby an allowance. If I give money to you or Patsy, I want a receipt. Is that clear?'

Yes.

Self-harm is a survival strategy. Self-harm represents extreme self-restraint.

Edward shows me where the vacuum cleaner is stored. He shows me the cupboard under the sink. Bathroom, scratched plastic bath, toilet, sink. White paint dots on these. The ceiling is white.

I ask Edward what he wants me to do.

Edward straightens his tie. 'You mean with Baby Girl? It says in the leaflet you have to pay attention to the injuries, show her that her body is worth caring about.'

'Do I stop her?'

'What does it say in the leaflet?'

I look at the leaflet.

'Do you own a mobile phone?'

'No.'

'Here's fifty. You can buy a mobile at the supermarket for almost nothing. I want change and a receipt.'

In the bathroom I look at the notes. A twenty, three tens. I use the toilet, flush, wash my hands. I dry my hands on Owl.

Edward hands me a sheet of notepaper. 'This is my number. Baby Girl has it too. Do not give it to Patsy. If I don't answer in three rings, I'm with my wife, will call you back. I do not text.'

I look at the number, or numbers, the digits.

Edward looks at his watch. 'I have to go. I have a meeting.'

I sit on the bed.

# 21

The barman wears a black shirt, the name of the pub on the pocket. The Red Lion Ealing, sewn.

Baby Girl is with her friend Alanna. Alanna is Baby's age. Alanna has straight black hair. The hair is long, touches her bottom.

We found the note on the green carpet. Baby left the note. Remove the cap, write it down. The pub name, the time. She wants us to meet her, Patsy said. I can tell from the handwriting.

The barman will not serve Baby Girl, Alanna.

'I'm eighteen,' Baby Girl says. 'She's nineteen,' pointing to Alanna.

The barman puts his hands on the bar. 'What's your date of birth?'

Baby Girl tells the barman a date.

The barman looks at the calendar. 'And your friend?'

Another date.

'Yes? And why would you know your friend's date of birth?'

Baby Girl shrugs.

'Birthday cards,' Alanna says.

'I only want orange juice anyway,' Baby says.

I order a pint of lager. For Patsy, tap water.

Along the bar, two men, suits.

'I'm learning,' one of the men says. 'I now know how to forward emails to another person and how to forward an email attachment.'

'It's about time,' the other man says.

'And somebody showed me how to get onto the internet. You click on something.'

We move to a table. The wood varnished dark brown. Ashtrays with the name of the brewery, Fullers.

Last night was the first night at Edward's flat. I slept on the bed with Patsy. Baby slept on the carpet. The carpet is snooker-table green.

Patsy dragged the cupboard away from the wall. Patsy is strong, has the strength of the mad. This is how Patsy describes herself.

Baby dreamt about Edward, uttered his name as she breathed. I stood over her as she breathed. The breath touched my face.

In the oblong space behind the cupboard, Baby Girl felt safe.

Baby Girl turns her back to the bar. Takes something from her knickers. A metal hip flask. Tips liquid into orange juice. 'Vodka. You can tell Edward if you like.'

I will not tell Edward.

At the bar, the men talk. 'West London is old money,' one of the men says. 'East London is new money.'

'Old Street is new money, perversely,' the other man says.

The men are old money.

We are no money. We have no money, nothing.

'Having said that,' one of the men says, then doesn't say anything else.

I find a newspaper on one of the chairs, *The Times*. There is a magazine, a supplement.

Baby leans across the table, touches my arm. 'Do you want us to kiss?'

No.

Baby Girl and Alanna kiss.

I look at my trainers, the wood.

Remove me from this world.

'We have to go to the toilet,' Baby Girl says.

The girls clang through doors. Whisper, shout, laugh. Voices bounce on tiles.

I instruct Patsy to follow.

From the table, I watch Patsy cross the pub to the toilet.

'They're in a cubicle together,' Patsy says when she returns. 'I told them I used to be a nurse and they laughed.'

Ten minutes. The toilet door opens. Alanna.

Alanna pulls out a chair, sits.

I do not think Baby Girl is cutting herself.

Patsy buys crisps. They do not have vole flavour. They do not have field-mouse flavour. Owl will have to make do with beef.

I unfold the newspaper, look at the back page.

'Rebecca doesn't tell me anything,' Alanna says. 'She's supposed to be my best friend.'

Patsy unzips her bag, tips the crisps onto Owl.

# 22

Edward's colleagues do not come here. They would not be seen dead in the Toby Jug. Edward tells me this. Edward's colleagues drink in Box.

I unfold the newspaper, drop it onto the table.

I ask Edward why his colleagues would not be seen dead in the Toby Jug.

'Look at the place,' Edward says.

I do this. The carpet is faded, sticky. Chewing gum, black with shoe dirt. Cigarette burns. Fruit machine. There are beer mats. On the screen, sport.

Edward puts the drinks on the table. Two pints of lager.

'We could go to Box.'

'My colleagues would see,' Edward says.

What would they see?

In the toilet, I look at myself in the mirror. I see what Edward's colleagues would see. T-shirt, jeans.

At the end of the bar, a woman is wrapped around a man. The woman is sitting on a high stool, her back against the wood. 'I might be quiet sometimes,' the woman says. 'You might come round and I might be like I was last night.'

I tell Edward to buy me a suit.

'You don't need a suit.'

'I want to get a job.'

Edward shakes his head. 'Why would you need a job? I'm not asking you for rent, Michael. Did you buy the mobile phone?'

I take the item from my jeans. I put the mobile phone on the table, with the newspaper.

'Does it have a camera?'

The mobile phone cost thirty pounds. The mobile phone does not have a camera.

'I have a spare mobile you can have. I think you just swap the SIM card. Did you keep the receipt?'

I did not keep the receipt. I invert my pockets.

'Let's try this a different way,' Edward says. 'Don't bother with receipts. I'll give you an allowance, like I do with Baby.'

I am not like Baby Girl. I tell Edward this.

Edward laughs. Booms into his pint. The shirt dark with lager. 'You are certainly not like Baby Girl. Do you know how old Baby Girl is?'

I do not know.

'Baby Girl is fifteen.'

I look at the newspaper.

'I have a daughter Baby's age. Has one of those iPod devices. Wanders around the house naked. Paints her toenails at the breakfast table. Do you want to know how I feel when I see that?'

I do not want to know.

'I want to fuck her. That is the truth, Michael. That is the reality of being a father.'

My finger moves. I touch the newspaper.

The *Daily Telegraph*, business section. The word BUSINESS, capital letters, a shadow effect on the letters. 1 Canada

Square, London. On the back page, Business Tomorrow.

Trader in legal battle sets up fund to manage personal wealth. Not authorised to manage client money.

Men in grey suits.

Edward takes out his mobile phone. It is shiny, a mirror. The surface reflects the face. Twisted, thin.

'Look at me, Michael. I am fifty-three years old. When I slip my finger inside Baby Girl, my finger is the finger of an old man.'

Baby, with Edward's finger inside her.

Baby Girl, a lolly on a stick.

'A difference of, what? Thirty-eight years?'

Edward counts the years. The daughter a baby, an infant, rolling on a fur rug. Edward stood at the foot of the stairs, his hand in his trouser pocket, rattling change.

You do not need me to take care of Baby Girl. You do not need me.

I say this to Edward.

I watch Edward's face.

Edward waves his hand. 'Forget all that. Why in hell do you read the financial pages?'

'I've read the other sections.'

'You said that last time, and I didn't believe you then. You don't need to impress me, Michael. It's not as though you want something from me.'

I do want something from you.

'I need a piss,' Edward says.

There are graphics, graphs. Statutory revenue, share price. Blue circle, red jagged line.

Share price 240p, 220p, 200p, 180p, 160p. This down the side.

J, A, S, O, N, D, J, F, M, A, M, J. These letters along the bottom. Who is Jason?

Companies. No, shares. Statutory revenue. General insurance 3.3%, Healthcare 32.4%, Banking 64.3%.

In the toilet, Edward shakes the drips.

I have a pen. Remove the cap, write it down. I write the figures in the margin.

$$3.3\%$$
$$32.4\%$$
$$64.3\%$$
$$\overline{\phantom{xxxx}}$$
$$100.0\%$$

The figures add up.

'Even I don't study that shit,' Edward says.

# 23

Owl is unwell. Woolly feathers have lost their sheen. Patsy brought him a dead vole and he wouldn't touch it.

The key turns in the lock. I hear this.

'Are you in?'

Yes. I am in bed with Patsy. Two, fully clothed. Trainers, boots like old-fashioned kettles.

Owl is under the bed, in the fluff and dust. Owl's tummy feathers collect dust. Every day, Patsy holds Owl at the window and brushes the dust from his tummy. The dust sails into the sky. Owl watches the dust. One day, Owl will fly away, and Patsy will cry.

In the hall, Baby talks to a young man. 'I just found ten pounds in my coat pocket,' Baby Girl says.

'Shall we get some cigarettes?'

'I wore that coat all day and I only just found it.'

I get out of bed.

Patsy sits up, props her back against pillows.

Baby Girl brings the man into the room. 'This is my boyfriend, Milo.'

Milo says hello. Milo looks around the room.

Hello.

Hello.

Baby Girl, what have you done?

I stand at the window.

Patsy tidies her petticoats.

Owl flutters, pecks. We hear this.

Milo has long hair. Through his ear, a tusk or bone. Milo has a tattoo. On Milo's T-shirt, words. ALIENATION, BOREDOM, DESPAIR.

Patsy wants to go to the pub.

'I've just taken my coat off,' Baby Girl says.

The pub is the Crown & Anchor. Cross the road, turn left. Past the gate where drunken businessmen urinate. Past the offices, the bank.

I look at the time on my supermarket phone. 19:24.

'These are on me,' Baby Girl says. In her hand, the note she found in her coat pocket. A crumpled brown leaf. Money that has died.

Baby Girl hides behind a wooden beam, behind Patsy.

With Baby's ten-pound note, Milo buys drinks.

| | |
|---|---|
| vodka and orange | £2.78 |
| Kronenberg | £2.90 |
| Carling Black Label | £2.85 |
| tap water | £0.00 |
| vole juice | n/a |
| | ——— |
| | £8.53 |

I write this on the corner of a newspaper. Remove the cap, write it down. Edward would not write this.

'Here,' Milo says. 'Your change.'

Baby looks at the coins, drops them into her coat pocket.

A couple touch thighs, laugh.

I look at the newspaper. A customer completed the cross-word, left. The customer left the newspaper on the table.

Milo is a student. Milo studies psychology. He studies computers, programming, neural networks.

Baby talks about a friend, a girl at her school. The girl cut herself. Dropped a glass of Coke into the bath. The glass broke. The glass invisible, the cloud brown and red. Reach in. Swirl.

I ask Baby Girl if Edward knows about Milo.

Milo is in the toilet. He cannot hear.

'No,' Baby says. 'I don't want to hurt him. You can tell him if you want.'

I will not tell Edward about Milo.

I move my hand from my pint. On the glass, in the condensation, the shape of a hand. The hand is my hand.

Patsy is worried about Owl.

I will fetch him.

I walk back to the flat. In the street, people. Silhouettes. The Tower of London. A man kicks a can.

In the flat, I reach beneath the bed.

I tuck Owl under my arm. You are safe.

Patsy is pleased to see Owl. Props him on her lap. Button eyes peer over the table. In his head, thoughts form, light as cotton cogs.

'There are more possible neuron connections in the human brain than atoms in the universe,' Milo says.

Owl, take notes.

Owl is an intellectual, a woolly scientist.

Milo buys ready salted crisps.

'Ready salted isn't a flavour,' Baby says. 'A flavour has to taste of something. Prawn cocktail is a flavour because it tastes of prawn.'

'Prawn cocktail crisps taste of sugar,' Patsy says.

Milo has a joke.

Two behavioural psychologists fucking. After they both come, one says to the other, 'It was good for you, was it good for me?'

Baby Girl laughs.

Baby has a joke, too.

'A man with a pumpkin for a head walks into a bar, orders a drink. The barman says, I hope you don't mind me asking, but how did you get a pumpkin for a head? There's a funny story behind that, the man says. I found a lamp, and when I rubbed it a genie appeared and granted me three wishes. For my first wish I wished for a harem of beautiful women. For my second wish I wished for a suitcase of money. This is all very interesting, the barman says, but how did you end up with a pumpkin for a head? So the man says, I was just coming to that. For my third wish, I wished for a pumpkin for a head.'

Milo opens his mouth, laughs. There are crisps.

Baby says the man who invented the joke was schizophrenic.

Patsy stuffs Owl into her bag. Stands, walks out.

'It wasn't that bad,' Milo says.

I follow Patsy into the street.

Here, by the wall, is Patsy. I stand behind Patsy. I put my arms around her waist, her heavy coat. I squeeze Patsy's tummy.

Patsy looks at bricks. Patsy puts her finger between bricks, to touch concrete.

I tell Patsy that the joke is not real. The joke has gone. The air conditioning sucked it in, chewed it up, spat it out.

Patsy thinks. Holds her hand to her mouth. 'What if the landlord had taken Owl?'

Owl is in your bag. Zipped up, safe.

'I am a very silly woman,' Patsy says.

No.

You are a confused woman.

A windswept Mary Poppins, blustery with rage.

# 24

Edward takes off his tie, hangs it over his chair, returns his hands to the table. 'All of the people I was close to died.'

'How many people?'

'A lot of people. A dozen in just six months. Michael, I was fourteen.'

'They all died together?'

'No,' Edward tells me. 'The incidents were unrelated. People who I shared significant parts of my life with. Three or four people.'

The Toby Jug, London Bridge. This time, Patsy is here. This time, Edward is drunk.

Edward's breath could wilt a flower.

Patsy has her hand in my lap. A rattish look in her eye. This is how Patsy describes herself.

I ask Edward how the people died.

'Unrelated. Differently.'

How?

'My friend Mark went first. There are two explanations. Mark had epilepsy. He took a lot of drugs, it could have been the drugs.'

Edward's wife called Edward at work. Edward's wife never calls Edward at work. Edward told me this.

Alicia found something in Edward's pocket, something to do with Baby Girl. This is why Alicia called Edward at work.

'Then there was Heidi, my girlfriend at the time. This was the most traumatic. Car crash. I saw the body. It was my job to identify her body.'

Edward put the phone down. Ended the call.

Edward drinking whisky. Sounds buzzed. Edward did not hear. Shoes up on the desk, swivel chair, slumped.

Edward's name on the office door. In the corridor, colleagues, afraid to knock.

'Then there was Matthew, a boy in my class.' Edward looks up from his hands. The hands are on the table. 'Matthew died of a rare illness. I forget the name. This is, what, thirty-nine years ago. I was fourteen, one year younger than Baby Girl. Boys made fun of him. Boys are not kind.'

'I want to wait outside,' Patsy says. Gets up, walks out of the pub.

'The last one was my aunt, Zara. Aunt Zara would care for me during the holidays. My parents would backpack around Asia.'

I ask Edward how Zara died.

'Prescription sleeping pills.' Edward straightens his back, his shoulders, the checked suit.

I do not care about Zara, Matthew, Heidi. I do not care about Mark. I care about Patsy, Owl. I care that Patsy is outside.

I want to invest in the stock market.

'No,' Edward says, shaking his head. 'None of this happened. I made it up.'

At the window, Patsy.

I wave, laugh.

Patsy bobs at the window. Opens the door.

Patsy sits with me, gulps water.

'I need people to feel sorry for me today,' Edward says. 'I'm drunk. And that is all.'

Edward's breath could bend coins. Edward's breath could cut glass.

'I will stay at the flat tonight,' Edward says, 'with you two and Baby.'

'And Owl,' Patsy says.

'And the owl, yes.'

# 25

Edward spins. 'What colours? Ask Baby Girl what colours.'

Patsy peers into the hall, through the doorway with no door. Baby Girl can do handstands. The soles of her feet lift from the carpet. The carpet is snooker-table green.

'What colours?'

Baby Girl peers between her legs. 'Depends what for.'

In the hall, I explain to Baby that Edward wants to re-decorate.

'It's too late. Tell him it's too late.'

Edward does not like this. 'Why is it too late?'

'It's midnight, Edward.'

'Oh. I thought you meant you would like to move out.'

Baby Girl does not want to move out.

'We can start tomorrow,' Edward says. 'What day is today? I can't think on whisky. What day was today, Michael?'

I do not know.

My days are boxes. Unlabelled, empty.

To Patsy and me, there is only today. Our time has stopped.

What day is it?

'A weekday,' Baby says to Edward. 'You went to work. I

had school but I didn't go.'

Owl will know. Owl is an intellectual.

On the windowsill, the leaflet. Understanding Self-Harm. Edward folds it, puts it into his suit pocket. 'Don't leave this lying around.'

Baby Girl does not cut herself. I tell Edward this.

'Michael, the girl has cuts all over her chest.' Edward faces the window, the darkening sky, the Tower of London. Edward takes the leaflet from his pocket, hands it to me. 'The truth may be far worse. Think about that.'

I hear Baby Girl land, skip to the front door.

I tell Edward I need money. I have worn the same pair of underpants for three days.

'Show me.'

I unbutton my jeans.

Do not touch me.

'I thought they might have cartoon characters on them.' Edward scratches his chin. Stubble, yellow fuzz. 'Why would your landlord confiscate your underwear?'

The landlord took all of our clothes. The landlord took Patsy's dressing-up box. I tell Edward this.

At the front door, Baby kisses Milo.

Alienation, boredom, despair.

Edward bangs his fist against the door frame, swears.

I walk down the hall. Baby kisses Milo on the lips. I tell Baby not to kiss Milo on the lips.

'Edward won't see.'

I talk to Baby. This, quietly. Do not upset Edward. We have to spend the night here. Four of us, and Owl. One bed, the floor, the bath. Edward scratching his thigh.

In Baby Girl's hand, the toy dog.

Patsy asks Milo to leave. And, he does leave.

'I'll text you tomorrow,' Baby Girl says.

Edward gives me money. 'A bottle of whisky and something to help me sleep.'

I put the money into my jeans pocket with the leaflet. Twenty pounds. Bank of England. I promise to pay the bearer on demand the sum of. Understanding Self-Harm.

Patsy holds my hand. We walk together.

'Owl doesn't like doors. Always banging in his face as he follows you around.'

Patsy

# 26

I walk with Baby Girl to the café. We walk on the pavement. Baby's kitten heels. My trainers, which I detest.

It has rained. The pavement is dark with fading rain.

I did not hear the rain. Patsy said that Owl heard it during the night. Owl is nocturnal. Owl is a night bird, an owl.

'Milo is meeting us,' Baby Girl says.

I did not know this. I thought it would be Baby, me. This is why I did not invite Patsy.

Edward and Baby Girl shared the bed. We slept on the snooker-table green carpet. Patsy used Owl as a pillow. Keep his tummy warm, Patsy said.

Today is Friday. Today, the carpenter will fit the doors. The bathroom, the lounge. Patsy will let him in. From the kitchen worktop, Owl will look down his beak, disapprove.

Tonight, Edward will go home to his wife, explain.

Tonight, Edward will tell a lie.

The café is called Green. Outside, the name of the café is painted on varnished wood. Inside, squishy chocolate-brown sofas, newspapers, people. Tables, chairs. Milo is sitting with his friends. The table is stacked with plates. On the top plate, olives, cheese.

Milo stands, kisses Baby Girl.

I turn away.

I sit at a table. I order sausage, chips.

Edward had a hangover. In the kitchen, while eggs boiled, Edward hatched a plan. He would be late for work, yes, but he would look immaculate. The taxi would stop at Hudson & Harvie in Jermyn Street. New shirt, new tie. The taxi would stop at M&S. Underpants, socks. The taxi would stop at Boots. Alka-Seltzer. Mouthwash, toothpaste, toothbrush. Deodorant, talc. Edward would wash at the swimming pool or gym.

The waitress circles my table.

Milo and his friends have eaten. There is some cheese left.

Baby Girl does not want to eat.

'Girls never eat,' one of Milo's friends says.

Edward will tell Alicia that he loves her. This is not the lie. The lie is Baby.

Baby Girl sits on Milo's lap. Milo lifts her up and down, pretending to fuck her.

Baby laughs.

If you fuck Baby Girl, you will go to prison.

'The sausages are vegetarian,' the waitress tells me.

Milo's friends are in a band. There are instruments.

Baby Girl wants to join the band.

'Can you sing?' one of Milo's friends asks.

'I sing in the bath.'

'We can't put a bath on stage,' the guitarist says. Behind his chair, the guitar. The guitar is in a canvas guitar case. In his mouth, a plectrum.

Edward would open the taxi window. Through the window, into a skip, these things. Edward will throw the objects. Mouthwash, toothbrush, toothpaste. Yesterday's underpants, shirt, tie, socks. Deodorant, talc.

The drummer taps the side of the table.

I wait, listen.

The waitress brings my breakfast.

'Sit with us,' Baby Girl says. 'This is Michael, my friend.'

The waitress helps me. Moves the stack of plates from the table, carries my plate to the table.

# 27

We had to get a taxi. Baby paid for the taxi with her allowance. The allowance is money received from Edward.

I wait with Baby Girl on the kerb. We watch the taxi pull away from the kerb.

In Baby's hand, change.

'I don't want the driver to know where he lives,' Baby Girl says. I do not know why she says this.

This is Hoxton Street, the market. Behind the shops, tower blocks. Today the market is not here. But there are remains.

The tower blocks rise above, like Owl.

'Ad's got a trendy loft,' Baby Girl says. Ad is the guitarist.

The flat is not on Hoxton Street. We turn off Hoxton Street, onto another street. Victorian warehouses converted into apartments. The street is lined with trees.

Baby Girl stops at a door, presses a button. We hear shoes.

Patsy would not get out of bed. This happened two days ago. Edward asked her why. Patsy missed her dressing-up box, her clothes. And Owl had a bib.

The lock is complicated. The door opens. Ad is standing behind the door. We can see half of Ad only. Half his grey sweatshirt, half his jeans. Ad is standing on the stairs.

Edward rescued Patsy's dressing-up box.

I follow Ad and Baby Girl up the stairs. Up three flights. Up, to Ad's loft.

Ad wears his jeans low. You can see his pants.

Ad has bought a product. X-Arcade. Relive the arcade experience at home. Ad lifts the product from the box. Manufactured from high-quality injected wood.

'Adam is into retro,' Baby Girl tells me.

Edward made a phone call on his mobile. This happened yesterday. Turned to Patsy, me. I need the landlord's name and address, Edward said.

The loft is huge. Spacious luxury apartment in London's fashionable East End.

We remove our coats.

Ad has friends here. Milo is here.

The product plugs into Milo's laptop. Authentic arcade feel, authentic arcade parts. The product is a computer joystick. On the CD, games.

If your landlord knows what's good for him, Edward said. These are big men.

We sit in Ad's loft and play games.

'Old school,' one of Ad's friends says.

Baby Girl sends me to get drinks. The drinks are in the kitchen, in the fridge. The fridge is lime green. On the front of the fridge, four letters, S M E G. I think the letters are magnets, you can move them, rearrange. The letters do not move. I touch the letters with my finger.

Inside the fridge, lager, Coke.

'Show Michael a card trick,' Baby Girl says to Ad.

Ad finishes his game, shifts over.

But there is something I want you to do for me, Edward said. There is something I want you to do for me. But not yet.

I put the drinks on the table.

I sit with Ad at the table. Ad has blond hair. In his hand, playing cards. AIR-CUSHION FINISH. MADE IN USA. Ad removes the cards from the box. Behind Ad, the window, the skyline, the sky.

Ad shuffles the cards. 'Name a card,' Ad says.

I name a card. The three of clubs.

Ad hands me the deck, asks me to find the three of clubs in the deck.

I spread the cards face up on the table.

I find the three of clubs.

'Close the deck face up and place the three of clubs on top.'

I do this.

Ad takes the deck, shuffles. Ad turns the deck face down, fans the cards. The backs of the cards are blue. 'Pick a card, any card. Don't let me influence you in any way.'

I try to pick a card, but Ad keeps fanning through the deck.

One of the cards has a red back. This makes me smile.

'Any one you like,' Ad says. 'A card that leaps out at you. A card that speaks to you.'

I point to the card with the red back.

'Turn it over.'

I turn the card over. The three of clubs.

I smile.

Baby claps her hands. 'He's brilliant,' Baby says.

We need to know each other better, Edward said.

Ad orders pizza. You can order on the internet. We play computer games until the pizza arrives.

I want to learn magic, like Adam. I will practise on Patsy. In Patsy's world, magic is real. In Patsy's world, everything is true.

# 28

'Alicia chose the venue,' a woman says. 'I wouldn't have held a party in an art gallery.'

'Don't be such a bitch,' another woman says.

'But I am a bitch.'

The women laugh.

I do not laugh.

A man brings food. The man is dressed as a fox, has a fox's tail. Fox hands are fingerless gloves, brown nail polish. The fox wears a waistcoat.

There is no music. A party, without music.

I want to sit in a room with Patsy. I will hold Patsy's hand. Patsy will not feel afraid.

A woman winks at the fox, picks a piece of food from the silver tray. The woman looks at me over her shoulder. 'Canapés,' the woman tells me.

The fox smiles a crafty fox smile.

The woman knows that I do not know what canapés are. I do not know how she knows this.

The woman takes canapés from the tray.

'Finger food,' the woman says. 'All canapés are finger foods, but not all finger foods are canapés.'

The fox trots away. Fox hoofs are brown suede shoes.

'These are broccoli quiche. And these are grilled shrimp and dill. I do the catering here.'

'You made them?'

'I didn't actually make them. The kitchen staff make them. Alicia and I were at catering school together. That's how we met. I'm Fiona.' The woman says this, holds out her hand.

We shake hands.

There is canapé on the woman's lip. The woman does not know this. I know this. The woman does not know that I know this.

'And you are?'

'Michael.'

'And how do you know Alicia?'

I do not know Alicia. I tell the woman this.

'You must meet her.' The woman taps a woman on the shoulder. The woman is Alicia. 'Alicia, this is Michael.'

Alicia is old. Seventy, eighty.

Alicia holds out her hand. 'Michael, how lovely to meet you.'

I nod.

I look around the room for Baby Girl.

Alicia turns away, talks to someone else, someone who talks.

I am an invader.

'Michael, say hello to Phil.' I turn to see Baby Girl standing by a painting. 'He did this painting.'

I look at the painting, at the man.

'It's a painting of a photograph,' Baby Girl says. 'You have to stand back.'

The man nods.

The man's beard is the colour of cement.

I stand back. I step away from the painting, into the room. The painting looks like a photograph.

'This is Michael, my boyfriend. Michael, meet Philip Hoard. He's related to Picasso, the famous painter.'

The man laughs. 'That's not actually the complete truth.'

'What is truth?' a man says.

Another man tells this man to shut up.

What is truth?

I do not know. I do not tell the truth.

Baby Girl holds my hand. Baby Girl is my girlfriend. We walk around the gallery. Together, we look at paintings.

Do not tell Patsy.

Do not tell Owl. Owl takes things too seriously. Owl has a tendency to overanalyse. It comes of being nocturnal, Patsy said.

'I want coke,' Baby Girl says.

I follow Baby into the toilet.

Girls stand by the mirror. No urinals. Sinks, cubicles. A plant.

I follow Baby Girl into one of the cubicles.

Baby lowers the toilet seat, unwraps the coke, tips it onto the seat.

'In America they call it a bump. I saw it in a film.' Baby says this as she chops the coke with her Oyster card. Baby does not have a credit card. Baby Girl is a child.

Baby snorts a line, or bump.

'Wow.' Baby stands up, breathes. 'Did you like those food things?'

I tell Baby that I did like them.

I tell Baby that I like her, that I like Baby Girl.

'I like you and Patsy too. And her owl. Do you like Yelper? Do you want a line?'

I do not want coke.

We return to the party.

Edward puts his arm around my shoulders, leads me to a woman. 'Alicia, this is the young man who fixed my computer. This is his girlfriend, Rebecca.'

'Mike, isn't it?'

'Michael.'

Alicia holds out her hand. 'Michael, how lovely to meet you. We have met before, but it's lovely to meet you again. Each time we meet it gets lovelier and lovelier.'

# 29

Baby Girl wants to be painted.

I buy two cans of Coke and sit with Baby Girl at the table. The café is Green.

At the party, a man gave Baby Girl his business card. The man is an artist. The man is not the artist who painted the painting that looks like a photograph.

Baby Girl shows me the card. On one side, a question mark. On the other, the artist's name, Daniel Lament. The words are painted. Daniel painted the words with a paintbrush. Daniel painted the telephone number.

'He makes his own business cards,' Baby Girl says.

Edward would not do this. I say this.

'Have you seen Edward's card?'

No.

Baby Girl stands, reaches into the back pocket of her skirt, takes out her purse. Baby wears pink. The skirt is made of felt. Sewn onto the front of the skirt, three pink feathers. The feathers have no meaning. The feathers are not like Owl's feathers. Owl's feathers do have meaning. Owl's feathers mean that Owl is a bird of distinction.

'We used to do painting at school,' Baby Girl tells me. 'We'd try to make the yuckiest colour we could, but it would always end up purple or brown.'

I nod.

'Or dark green. You'd think it would make black.'

Black is not a colour. Black is no colour.

Baby Girl puts her purse on the table. Baby's purse is made of denim. Patsy's purse is made of silk. Edward does not own a purse. Edward is a man, a businessman. Edward's wallet is made of leather.

Baby takes Edward's business card from her purse, puts it on the table. Edward's business card looks expensive. The letters are gold. The card is thick, off white.

'I need a pee.' Baby stands as she says this. 'Michael, will you come with me?'

I look at the toilet door. On the toilet door, the shape of a woman. The woman on the toilet door is not Baby Girl.

Baby laughs. 'Not to the toilet. To watch Daniel Lament paint my portrait.'

I look at the toilet door, at the artist's business card.

The business card is a door.

# 30

Time to throw things out, Patsy says. Time for a change.

But Patsy does not like change.

Owl thrives on change. Owl is an anarchist. When the revolution comes, Owl will fly up to his nest. Owl does not like to get his claws dirty. Owl likes to wait in the wings.

Patsy tosses clothes. I sit on the bed, behind Patsy. The clothes land on me, the bed, the floor.

Dresses, petticoats, skirts.

Cowboy hat.

Boots.

Stripy socks.

Clogs.

I ask Patsy if these are the things she is throwing out, or the things she is keeping.

'I'm taking everything out of the trunk first. Things I want to keep I'll put back in.'

The trunk is Patsy's wooden dressing-up box.

Knickers, stockings. Lace. These items land on me.

A red plastic belt. More belts, leather.

Trainers.

Empty canvas bag.

Owl's nappy. This from when Owl was a baby owlet.

What do I own? I do not know. I look around the flat.

The supermarket mobile phone I bought with Edward's money.

Trainers, jeans, some T-shirts, sweatshirts, jacket.

I do not own a suit.

I have no laptop, no computer equipment. The landlord took the computer, the iPods. Patsy called them the magnificent seven.

No records, CDs, DVDs.

Keys to this flat.

I have money. Coins, notes. I put Edward's money into my pocket. I do not own a wallet.

I have a souvenir coin. Elizabeth II, GRA REG FID DEF. I do not know what this means. I turn the coin in my hand. Edward would invest the coin in the stock market. Ad would make the coin vanish. The coin has a diagram. DNA DOUBLE HELIX. The words are in capital letters. 1953 TWO POUNDS 2003. The coin is three years old. I am thirty, the same age as Patsy. Baby Girl is fifteen. Owl is two.

I watch Patsy sort through the clothes. This to keep, this to keep.

Patsy reaches into the bottom of the trunk. Touches the wood with her hand.

I stand up from the bed. I open a kitchen cupboard. Spacious studio in the City. Inside the cupboard, crisps, tinned soup, pasta, onions, noodles, jars of sauce, jars of olives. Liquorice. I bought the liquorice for Owl.

I ask Patsy if she wants crisps. Yes. I throw two packets of crisps onto the bed, the clothes.

I sit on the bed, eat.

Patsy says liquorice tastes like vole blood. Owl told her this. And Owl should know.

'These are the things I'm keeping,' Patsy says.

Into the trunk, these things. Patsy throws the things. Dresses, petticoats, skirts. Cowboy hats, boots. Socks, clogs. Stockings, knickers. Belts, trainers. Empty canvas bag.

Time to throw things out, time for a change. But Patsy does not like change.

What are you throwing out, Patsy?

Patsy closes the wooden trunk. Sits on the trunk. In Patsy's hand, Owl's nappy. This, from when Owl was a baby owlet. Patsy tells me this. Owl grew out of nappies when he started university.

# 31

Baby Girl wants her friend to do it with her.

I ask Baby Girl which friend.

'Alanna with the long hair, who you met in Ealing.'

Yes, I say. I remember.

Baby Girl wipes something from her seat, sits down. The seats are made of plastic, metal.

The café is on Old Street. Patsy said the café is a greasy spoon.

Patsy is outside, smoking an imaginary cigar. I do not know why Patsy is doing this.

On the window, words. The words are in reverse. I can see the words on the glass. RITAS' CAFE. The apostrophe is in the wrong place.

I ask Baby Girl what she wants her friend to do with her.

'The portrait. I just phoned Daniel Lament.'

Baby made the call outside. I watched Baby Girl through the window. To the left of the E stood Baby Girl, talking into her mobile phone. To the right of the R stood Patsy, the cigar. The cigar is not real.

I look at the table, at the objects on the table. There are ashtrays. The ashtrays are made of tin foil. Our ashtray is empty. The ashtray at the next table contains cellophane, cigarette butts, ash.

Patsy comes in, sits beside Baby Girl.

I ask Patsy why she went outside to smoke an imaginary cigar.

'Owl smokes cigars. I don't want the police to take him.'

Baby Girl asks Patsy if Owl's cigars are imaginary.

'No. Owl smokes real cigars.'

Owl does smoke real cigars. Owl's cigars are imported from Cuba.

'I have to call Alanna,' Baby Girl says.

Patsy reaches across the table for my hand. We hold hands.

'I thought you were going to call her,' Patsy says.

'I'm texting her instead. I don't want to talk about art in a place like this.'

I look around the café. The men here are not artists. They are lorry drivers, builders. There is a man in uniform. The men want to touch Baby Girl.

# 32

'There are never riots these days,' Ad says.

Milo switches off the television.

Ad picks up his guitar, holds it in his lap. In Ad's mouth, the plectrum.

I sit on the sofa with Patsy.

'Michael can be roadie,' the drummer says.

I am not big enough to be roadie. Patsy can be roadie.

'We need a cultural revolution,' Ad says.

'That's the problem,' the bass player says. 'We don't need a revolution. People are happy. People are complacent.'

Baby Girl's mobile phone rings. Baby looks at the screen, presses a button. The sound stops.

The band set up the instruments.

'Self-expression isn't the point,' Ad says. 'It shouldn't be a statement. We need to make an anti-statement.'

Baby sends me to get drinks. I walk to the kitchen. Socks on wood, tiles. Four letters, S M E G. Inside the fridge, lager, Coke.

From the other room, sounds. The drums, the drum kit. Ad tunes the guitar.

Baby Girl walks into the kitchen. 'I wish Edward would leave me alone,' she tells me.

I want Edward to call me.

I want to know what index linked means.

All work is boring, Edward said. If you want to do it, it isn't work.

Ad shows me how to use his Mac, how to connect to the internet. I am a PC person, Ad is a Mac person.

Baby Girl's mobile rings.

I look up Smeg on the internet. Ad's fridge cost a lot of money. When I get a job, I will buy a Smeg fridge.

In my hand, numbers scrawled on a piece of paper. Remove the cap, write it down. My chest size, my waist size. Inside leg.

Baby sits on her phone. The sound rises from beneath Baby Girl's legs.

I search for suits. I find a website that sells suits mail order. This while the band rehearse, discuss. I find a suit that is checked, like one of Edward's.

You need a credit card. Or, a debit card. My bank account is closed. This due to bankruptcy.

Baby finds her bag, her purse. Inside the purse, a credit card. The credit card is Edward's.

'I use it all the time,' Baby Girl says.

I input numbers.

I type the address of Baby's flat. Spacious studio in the City. The box will arrive. I will open the box.

Baby Girl wants Ad to show me another card trick.

'Grab a beer,' Ad says.

I walk to the kitchen in socks paid for by Edward. I take a can of Carlsberg, walk back to the lounge.

I sit with Ad at the table. Ad has blond hair. In his hand, playing cards. BICYCLE RIDER BACK. Ad removes the cards from the box.

Ad shuffles the cards, fans the cards. 'Pick a card,' Ad says.

I pick a card.

'Look at it, and place it on top of the deck.'

I look at the card. The eight of hearts. I place the card on the top of the deck. The card is face down.

Ad squares up the deck. 'Give the cards a quick shuffle and hand them to me.'

I shuffle the cards. I am not good at this.

'Now,' Ad says, taking the deck, 'if I tap the cards like this, your card rises to the top. Turn over the top card.'

I turn over the top card. The eight of hearts.

Ad turns the card face down, squares the deck and hands the deck back to me. 'This time, shuffle them really well. Lose your card deep in the deck.'

I shuffle the cards.

'Keep shuffling. If you shuffle a card deep into the deck you can lose that card forever. Spread them face up on the table and see if you can find your card.'

I turn the deck over and spread the cards on the table.

The eight of hearts is not on the table.

I smile.

'That's impossible,' Baby Girl says.

Patsy shrugs. The sky is pink, the clouds are blue.

'Owl has to go to such lengths to amuse himself in the city. Mind you, it's the same in the countryside for humans.'

Patsy

# 33

Edward said just me.

Not Baby Girl.

Not Patsy.

Me.

Beyond the window, trees wag their fingers.

There are newspapers. The newspaper rack is knitted wicker. The restaurant is not like Alicia's Rooms. This restaurant is not modern. Alicia's Rooms does not have newspapers.

I follow the waiter to the table.

Edward looks up from his open briefcase.

I sit, read the newspaper.

Integrated support. Fell $\frac{1}{2}$p to $9\frac{1}{2}$p. It also raised 3.4m in a placing of 48.5m new shares at 7p each to strengthen its balance sheet.

On the table, a checked tablecloth. The check is not like the check on Edward's suit. It is not like the check on my suit.

'Sautéed pigeon breast with red wine gravy.'

I want this too. I tell the waiter this.

I tell Edward I need the toilet. This is true. Though, I do not need to urinate.

In the mirror, myself, my suit. It is wrong.

I walk back to the table, pull out my chair, sit.

Edward looks at me.

I scratch the back of my head. Behind my head, a door. I saw the door when I sat down. The chair and table block the door.

'This is creepy,' Edward says. 'It doesn't even fit. Where did you get it?'

'The internet.'

'You ordered a suit over the internet?'

I nod. I did do this.

'If you want a suit that badly, Michael, I will buy you a suit.'

Edward looks at figures. Shuffles papers. To me, the figures are upside down. To me, the figures have no meaning.

We do not speak.

Edward pours more wine, tops up my glass.

We study figures. We do not speak.

The waiter brings our food.

'Another bottle of red,' Edward says.

I fold my newspaper. I do not know where to put it. I place the newspaper in my lap. If I drop sautéed pigeon breast or spill red wine gravy, it will land on the newspaper.

Edward looks at me. Edward has chewed it over. Edward is ready to speak. 'Why won't Baby Girl take my calls?'

I do not know.

'Michael?'

'I don't know.'

Edward puts down his knife and fork, folds his arms on the tablecloth. 'Baby Girl has a boyfriend.'

I nod.

'Am I right? She has a boyfriend?'

'Yes.'

Edward pushes his plate.

Owl swoops in through the window, grabs the pigeon meat from Edward's plate, drags it onto the floor.

'I didn't know anything about this. That was a guess. Why didn't you tell me?'

Owl, leave us.

Owl ruffles his tail feathers, hops onto the windowsill, spreads his woolly wings and soars off into the open air.

A gentleman knows when he's not wanted.

Waiter, clean up this mess. Forgive Owl. He was born in a barn.

Edward looks unwell. 'I want you to separate them. Michael, if you successfully terminate this relationship, I will take you to Hardy & Skinner to fit you for a suit.'

I look down at my suit.

At the window, trees bow their heads.

I tell Edward about the loft in Hoxton. Spacious luxury apartment in London's fashionable East End. Smeg fridge. I tell Edward about the band. There is space to rehearse. The drummer sets up the drum kit.

Edward turns green, turns away.

Edward drinks his wine.

I tell Edward about the card trick. The card disappeared. The card changed colour.

'That's all I need. Cast aside for a fucking wizard.'

No. The magician is Adam. Baby's boyfriend is Milo, a psychology student. Milo has a tattoo. Milo has a tusk or bone through one ear. There are more possible neuron connections in the human brain than atoms in the universe. Milo said this.

Like Owl, Milo is an intellectual. Unlike Owl, Milo eats from a plate.

'I want photographs of this boy's flat.'

The flat is Adam's.

'Do you have your phone?'

Yes.

Edward takes his mobile phone from his pocket. 'This is the spare phone. It wasn't expensive but it does have a camera. You can swap the SIM card.'

I take the supermarket phone from my pocket, unclip the back, remove the SIM card, insert it into Edward's phone.

'You can throw that cheap one away.'

I drop the supermarket phone onto my plate.

Edward laughs. 'How are we going to do this?'

This is a meeting. This is a deal.

I think, eat.

I tell Edward my idea.

Baby Girl has a laptop. I will send Milo an email from Baby's email address. Milo will think that the email is from Baby Girl.

'You're going to hack into Baby's email account?'

I nod.

I need these things. I tell Edward the things.

A pen drive to transfer software onto Baby's laptop. An internet connection at the flat.

Edward looks at the trees.

# 34

The man installed the telephone line. This happened this morning. Cut a hole in the wall. Fitted cables. Fitted the socket.

While the man worked, Baby slept. I looked at Baby Girl on the bed. Patsy looked at me.

The man held his back, complained.

Owl detests the working classes. Yet he claims to be a Marxist.

I offered the man eggy bread. Owl offered the man a dead bat. The man from BT was not hungry.

How thick is a bat's wing? A bat's wing is one cell thick. This according to Owl's encyclopaedia.

Owl does not eat the wing. Spits it out. The best part of a bat, Owl tells us, is the guts.

While the man worked, I cuddled Patsy in the bathroom.

The man tested the line with an electronic device.

Beep.

Yes, we are live.

The man left.

This happened this morning. Now, it is not morning.

I show Baby Girl the telephone socket. BT installed it while you slept. The man saw your knickers, the soles of your feet. We watched you move on the bed. I do not tell Baby this.

I tell Baby that we have internet.

'Can I check my emails?'

Yes. I will set up the connection.

Baby reaches under the bed for her laptop. I plug the cable into the laptop, into the wall.

The fastest broadband on the planet, Edward said. I want Baby's friends to be impressed.

Broadband takes weeks. You sign up, you wait.

Instead, dial-up, 56Kbps.

Owl shakes his beak in disgust.

# 35

Ad's sofa is chocolate brown, squishy.

I take photographs of Adam's sofa. I take photographs while Ad and Milo play cards.

I photograph the shelf, the playing cards.

I photograph the skyline, the sky.

I photograph the Smeg fridge. Four letters, S M E G. The fridge is lime green.

These photographs, with Edward's mobile phone.

Outside, I took photographs of Ad's street, the trees, the front door. I took photographs of the market in Hoxton Street.

I photograph the business page of the newspaper. This for no reason. I bought the newspaper at the newsagent on Hoxton Street. Patsy waited outside, with Owl. Don't lose him, I said. If you lose Owl, you will never find him again, and you will weep buckets.

When I came out of the newsagent, Patsy was crying.

Have you lost Owl?

No. He is here.

Don't think about it. Think about sunshine, cake.

Do not put ideas into Patsy's head.

Ad is into retro. Ad has a game, Twister. 'It came out in

the sixties,' Ad says. 'The man who patented it nicked the idea from a kid.'

On the box, a photograph. The photograph shows a family playing Twister. Hands, feet on coloured circles. The game that ties you up in knots.

Ad shows us the bedroom. The duvet is a Twister duvet. The duvet is white with coloured circles. Green, yellow, red, blue. On the pillows, red Twister logo. 'That duvet got me laid so many times.'

'Are you being ironic?' the bass player says.

'Irony is dead,' Ad says. 'Sincerity is the new irony.'

Baby Girl laughs.

I do not take photographs in Adam's bedroom.

In the lounge, Ad opens the box, lifts the lid, places the lid on the table.

Ad takes items from the box. Here are the items. Ad puts the items on the floor. Cardboard spinner, plastic sheet. On the sheet, circles. Green, yellow, blue, red.

The spinner is divided into sections. Left Foot, Right Hand, Left Hand, Right Foot.

'What if you're left handed?' the drummer says.

Baby Girl sends me to get drinks. In the kitchen, I open the lime green fridge, take out four cans, close the fridge door.

We spread the mat on the floorboards. If you are playing outside, anchor the corners with your shoes. It says this in the instructions.

Patsy does not want to play. 'Not with my big bum,' Patsy says.

Ad, Milo, Baby Girl, me.

'Everyone keep your socks on,' Ad says.

The bass player spins the spinner. The plastic arrow moves. The arrow points to a body part, a colour.

Left hand, blue.

Right hand, yellow.

I reach for a blue circle with my left hand. I reach for a yellow circle with my right hand. My face is near Baby Girl's thigh. Baby Girl is wearing orange tights, red shorts, white vest.

Right hand, green.

Left foot, red.

If the move is impossible or will cause you to fall, you may eliminate yourself from the game.

Baby Girl falls, rolls onto her back, laughs.

Right foot, yellow.

I fail, flail, fall.

Where is Patsy? I look around the flat. I look in the kitchen, the bedroom. I tap on the bathroom door. Patsy is in the bathroom, her bag open. Owl looks at me from the sink.

'Owl's birthday,' Patsy says.

Today is Owl's birthday. And that means bath day.

Patsy washes rodent stains from Owl's feathers. The water is brown, soapy. I sit on the edge of the bath. I watch as Patsy changes the water.

# 36

In the corner, Baby Girl's bag. The bag is pink, with butterflies.
I unzip the bag, look inside. I remove items.

Knickers.

Vests.

Socks.

Chocolate bars, crisps.

Yelper, Baby Girl's tiny toy dog.

Phone charger. The cable has been repaired with a strip of
black tape. Patsy burnt the cable with a candle.

Nail polish. Three bottles. Hard Candy, pink. Rimmel
Nail Lacquer, brown. Boots No7 Colour Lock Nail Enamel,
red. I unscrew the top, look at the brush. This brush has
touched Baby's toes.

Tissues. Baby Girl blew her nose. I put the tissues into my
pocket.

Spare laces for Baby's trainers.

Hotel matches.

Another tissue, with lipstick, red. I have no interest in
this.

A notebook. Baby Girl has drawn a picture of Yelper.
Baby has drawn a picture of Owl. Patsy will like this
picture. I will tell Patsy about the picture, then tell Patsy

that I did not tell her about the picture. In Patsy's world, everything is true.

Mints.

Baby's watch. The strap is dirty from Baby's skin.

Vitamin tablets in a plastic pot. It is important, we are told. You have to look after yourself.

A key ring, no keys.

I listen, aware of sounds.

Edward looked at the photographs. I took the photographs on the mobile phone. The photographs show Ad's flat. The front door, the floorboards, the wall. The posters on the wall.

I did not know why Edward wanted the photographs. Now, I do know.

Spacious studio in the City.

Edward decorated the flat to look like Ad's flat.

The flat has new doors. The man who fitted the doors returned to fit new doors. The doors are like the doors in Ad's flat.

There are posters. The posters are not the same as the posters in Ad's flat. Let's not make it obvious, Edward said. I want to create the feel, not a facsimile.

Edward did not decorate the flat. Edward paid men.

In the kitchen, a fridge, Smeg. Not lime green. Let's not make it obvious. The fridge is pink. Unlike Ad's fridge, this fridge contains food. Edward sent Patsy to the supermarket.

Outside, shouting. I hear this.

I put these things back into Baby Girl's bag, zip the bag closed. Beneath the bag, a black canvas case. I lift the bag onto the bed and open the case.

Baby Girl's laptop.

Baby's computer is a PC. The lid is metallic blue. I open the lid. The screen is dusty. Between the keys, tobacco.

Like me, Baby is a PC person.

Patsy is a pen and paper person. Remove the cap, write it down.

Owl is not a person. Owl is an owl.

Owl cannot use a keyboard. His wings get in a flap.

Patsy and Baby Girl will not return for two or more hours.

Outside, traffic.

In my pocket, a pen drive. Plug it in, transfer data. On the pen drive, key logging software. I downloaded the software at an internet café. I plug the pen drive into the USB port on the side of Baby's laptop. I install the software on Baby's laptop.

To test the program, I open a document and type a series of letters, qwertyuiop. I locate the key-logger folder and open the log file. The file contains the date, the time, 13.51, and the series of letters, qwertyuiop.

# 37

'We tend to think bespoke and made to measure are the same, but this is incorrect.'

Edward tells me this. I listen.

'We're going to be in there a while. Do you know how many measurements they take, Michael? Upwards of twenty. It's not just under the arms and inside leg.'

The street is called Savile Row. The taxi drove down Piccadilly, Regent Street.

I listen to Edward.

'A made-to-measure suit is based on a template pattern. The bespoke pattern is designed from scratch.'

The driver talks about his family. I am not interested. I listen to Edward.

The driver opens a can of Coke.

Twenty-five thousand roads, the driver tells us. There are twenty-five thousand roads in London. No grid system. No standard template.

On the pavement, we watch the taxi drive away.

I walk in through the door. Edward holds the door.

Edward smiles.

Edward's shoes have heels. I wear trainers.

There are four people involved in the making of a suit.

Edward told me this in the taxi. I watched Edward's lips. Tailor, coat maker, trouser maker, finisher. Felling means sewing. Then, Edward looked out of the window.

'May I help?'

Yes. You may help.

The man is a tailor. The tailor has his hands in his pockets. Tape measure, chalk. Maroon tie, blue pinstriped suit.

The suit will cost £1,940. Price does not include VAT.

'Fine,' Edward says.

The tailor has sandy hair, a moustache. With spectacles and beaky nose, the tailor resembles Owl.

Owl joined a gentleman's club. The club is called the Pecking Order. The owls discuss their favourite vole sauce. Buttery, peppery, plain.

At Owl's club, the tailor would be most welcome.

'The buttons will be made from animal horn,' the tailor says.

Edward smiles, pleased.

There are shears. The shears look like mangled metal. The shears were made by a blacksmith, a friend of the tailor. The tailor is proud of the shears. With one hand behind his back, the tailor tells us this.

We discuss posture, style.

The tailor asks where I intend to wear the suit.

'In an office,' I say.

Edward looks away.

The tailor uses words that I would not use, words that Owl would use. Diligence, meticulous.

'We do a lot of tweaking,' the tailor says. 'One cannot tell.'

# 38

'Patsy, the fruitcake,' Edward says.

Patsy is not a fruitcake.

Owl is a fruitcake. Plump, brown, round. Owl eyes are two currants.

I tell Edward I need a job.

'You don't need a job,' Edward says.

'I do need a job.'

'I need you to take care of Baby Girl. She cuts herself.'

I shake my head. I do not believe this. I do not say this.

I tell Edward that Patsy will look after Baby Girl.

The pub is called the Lamb. The pub is in a back street off Savile Row. Men here wear suits, like Edward.

'We've gone through this,' Edward says.

'You can't stop me.'

'No, but I can evict you from the flat. You and that Patsy.'

And Owl.

'If I get a job I won't need your flat.'

'Yes, if you live in zone thirteen. Rent in London is prohibitively expensive. You might end up in the suburbs, in the cupboard under someone's sink.'

The wood is dark brown, varnished. This pub is clean. On the wall, pictures, brass.

'Young people in London work the longest hours in Europe. You would think they would be handsomely rewarded, Michael. Most of these people cannot afford to eat. They certainly cannot afford luxuries.'

I watch Edward sip his lager. The jacket sleeve moves down the arm. I look at Edward's watch.

I look at my lager. I do not drink.

'That was an exaggeration, Michael. But they won't be able to live in the City. These people who work more hours than they sleep. How many people do you know who own a Smeg fridge?'

'Adam.'

'He probably conjured it up with his magic. I expect his parents bought it. A boy that age can't afford to spend nine hundred quid on a refrigerator.'

I tell Edward I need the toilet.

Edward watches me as I cross the pub.

In the toilet, an old man. He urinates, washes his hands with soap. The man will not touch the door handle. 'A lot of men don't wash their hands,' the man says. The man holds the door handle with the cuff of his shirtsleeve. The man cannot open the door. Steps back. 'Be a gentleman,' the man tells me.

I will be a gentleman.

I open the door.

In the mirror, my face, the top of my T-shirt.

Soon, I will not wear a T-shirt, a suit ordered over the internet, trainers. I will wear a bespoke suit, a shirt, a tie. I will be a gentleman, like Edward and Owl.

I do not need the toilet.

Edward watches me walk back to the table.

'Posture,' Edward says.

I straighten my back, sit.

'Posture,' Edward says again.

I straighten my back in the chair. My shoulder blades touch the back of the chair, or the wooden panel behind the chair.

Edward rolls my sweatshirt into a ball, wedges it between my lower back and the back of the chair. 'Like this. Look at me.'

I look at Edward.

The couple at the next table argue. That was what I meant. No, that was not what you meant. That was what I meant. The man folds his arms. Then say so.

At the bar, Edward buys crisps, pork scratchings. Edward offers the pork scratchings to me.

No. I want the crisps.

The woman grabs her handbag, walks out. The man rubs his chin.

Edward recognises a man. Not one to forget a face.

I recognise the man too. The man is the man from the toilet, the man who washed his hands with soap.

Edward straightens his back. 'He may ask you how you and I know each other. Don't let on.'

I look at the table, the pale rings.

The man recognises Edward. 'How funny to run into you,' the man says. 'I just had lunch with Alicia.'

'Jeremy is friends with my wife,' Edward tells me.

I nod.

'In a city of this size,' the man says, sitting at our table. 'I have a bottle of wine.' The man stands again, crosses the pub to a table, carries the bottle and the glass back to our

127

table. The bottle is dark green, or bottle green. The man pours red wine into the glass.

The man wears a pink shirt, a suit. The suit is brown.

'I collect coincidences,' the man tells me. 'I'm writing a book.'

Edward nods.

'He thinks I'm joking,' the man says to Edward.

I do not think that the man is joking.

'This one won't go in the book. We need something more substantial.'

'We could fabricate it,' Edward says.

'Yes. I had lunch with your wife, then I bumped into you, and you and I were wearing the exact same socks.'

Edward laughs.

I nod, smile.

'Jeremy, this is Michael.'

'Hello, Michael.'

We shake hands. Hello.

The man puts his glass to his lips, peers into the glass, over the glass, at me. 'Do you know how Edward and Alicia met?'

No.

'There was a coincidence involved in the meeting. Or was there?'

Edward shakes his head. He does not want Jeremy to tell the story.

'Alicia was Edward's home economics teacher. Edward would have been fifteen. Would that be right?'

Jeremy looks at Edward.

Edward looks at a pork scratching.

'Alicia was Edward's teacher, Michael. They had some

sort of affair. Alicia's my age so she must have been fifty, give or take a year. Not that one can afford to do so at fifty.'

'Jeremy, please.'

'They were caught together in the crockery cupboard. Edward had his hand down her underwear.' Jeremy looks at Edward. 'Or was it the other way around?'

'Jeremy, stop.'

Edward drinks some of his lager. Lowers his chin to the glass. Posture, Edward.

'Alicia talks about it a lot. I find your marriage quite fascinating. I find myself obsessing over it.' Jeremy looks at me. 'It's funny the obsessions people have, isn't it.'

I nod.

Jeremy finishes his glass, pours another. 'I should call Alicia, tell her we're in here.'

'No point,' Edward says. 'We have to get back to work.'

We stand.

'Surely you have time to finish your drinks?'

We look at our drinks.

Edward sits, drinks.

I do not sit. I do not drink.

The man wags his finger. 'How do you two know each other?'

Edward looks at me, at himself. 'Um. Work.'

I look at my trainers.

'Michael works in the post room,' Edward says.

Jeremy slaps the table with his hand. 'I knew it. You work with my grandson, Agustine.'

Agustine?

'My daughter-in-law is Irish. It means majestic. Agustine works in the post room too.'

'At which company?'

'At your company, Edward. You're still at Young City Investments, yes?'

Edward nods. Coughs.

'My grandson works there. You did know this.'

Edward remembers, nods.

I tell Edward that I do know Agustine.

'This is remarkable,' Jeremy says. 'I told you I collect coincidences. It's one for the book.' Jeremy empties his wine glass, fills it, empties the bottle. 'If I ever write it. I am eighty-eight years old. Can you believe that? The same age as Alicia. Is that right?'

Edward nods.

'I must say, it's very noble of you to drink with a post-room boy, Edward. No offence to you, Michael.'

'Michael offered to fix Alicia's computer,' Edward says.

'Perhaps Michael can fix my computer.'

'We have to leave,' Edward says. 'Goodbye, Jeremy.'

'We must do lunch.'

'Yes.'

Edward places our pint glasses on the bar. One empty, one full.

'Owl hired a sparrow to do his dirty work. Probably paid him half a stick of liquorice for his efforts, knowing how tight Owl is.'

Patsy

# 39

Edward wants Baby Girl to buy stickers. Coloured stars, pink hearts.

'I'm too old for that sort of thing,' Baby Girl says.

Edward is hurt.

'Owl stickers,' Patsy says. In Patsy's hand, a sheet of stickers. Each sticker depicts an owl. Every sticker is different. In Patsy's bag, Owl. Patsy unzips her bag, shows the stickers to Owl.

'I love Owl,' Baby Girl says.

A couple walk past. The man points to Patsy's skirts. The couple whisper, laugh.

This is Patsy's fairytale princess outfit. The tiara, the lacy gloves. The charming silver detail. Gold coins in a silk purse.

Patsy sticks an owl sticker to Owl's woolly tummy.

Oh yes, Owl. Very fetching. It suits you down to the claws.

Don't patronise me, Owl says.

Crystal Stickers. 1 sheet. Decorate walls, furniture, windows, exercise books, gifts. Owls are not mentioned.

'You have to buy them,' I say.

Patsy takes two gold coins from her purse.

I tell Patsy not to buy the stickers.

Patsy drops the coins into her purse. Chink, chink.

I take the sticker sheet from Patsy, return it to the hook.

I hear Edward say to Baby Girl, 'I want you to be my little girl.'

Baby Girl shakes her head. No.

We walk out into the street. The pavement is damp. The air is damp.

Owl is a shoplifter. On his tummy, an owl sticker.

Edward has something to say.

I walk with Edward.

'I've arranged for you to work at Young City Investments,' Edward says. 'Just for a few weeks. You will work in the post room, with Jeremy's grandson.'

Edward looks at Baby Girl. Baby Girl is walking ahead, with Patsy. They walk on the pavement. They cross the road. Baby Girl looks back.

Above, sky, clouds.

# 40

Ad says he is thinking of becoming a misogynist. 'When I was eight, this girl threw stones at me in the playground, and when we went in she told the teacher it was me who threw stones at her.'

'What's that got to do with misogyny?' Milo says.

'She was a woman, and she got me detention.'

'Ad, she was eight years old.'

Ad laughs, drinks coffee.

'Maybe you should hate children,' Milo says.

'Or detention,' Baby Girl says.

'Or stones,' Patsy says.

I squeeze Patsy's hand.

I say something about being tired. I cannot remember.

Milo tells me to drink caffeine.

At the counter, I buy a can of Coke. The café is called Demur. The name is odd. The café is in Shoreditch. In Shoreditch, the name is not odd.

Wooden floors, wooden ceilings, wooden window frames, wooden tables, wooden seats. The plates are yellow. The toilet doors are painted yellow.

'Caffeine takes half an hour to work,' Milo says.

The bassist and drummer are here. I listen to them talk.

The bassist and drummer discuss the band.

'We should challenge everything,' the bassist says. 'The way things work in the band, the way things work with the audience. Everything.'

'How do we do that?'

'That's the point of challenging things.'

I could not sleep. Owl kept me awake. Owl kept pecking me.

There is a girl here. The girl is talking to the drummer. 'I got together with a friend of Adam,' the girl says.

'What friend?'

The girl tells the drummer the name. I do not hear the name. 'He tried to pull me when we were out clubbing. We were chatting and I told him I was off my head and he tried to snog me.'

The drummer nods. Drums on the table with his hands.

'Then, last weekend, he said we should go to my house for a lay down, and we did.'

Patsy stares at the window, through the window, at a bus. On the side of the bus, an advert.

My eyes close.

'He kept trying to get me to sleep with him,' the girl says. 'In the morning we were chatting in bed and I touched his shoulder and he pulled away.'

'Then what?' the drummer says.

The girl shrugs. 'Why would you want to sleep with a girl you don't even want to touch?'

The drummer does not know. Looks at the bassist, at Milo, Ad.

I look out of the window. Another bus, another advert.

'I've never had sex,' Baby Girl says.

'I don't like it,' the girl says. 'You might like it, but I don't.'

# 41

'The shredder is in this corner. You turn it on. The paper goes in the top.'

The man flicks a switch. There is no sound. The man counts six sheets, inserts them into the machine. There is sound, noise. 'Six is the most it will take at one time.'

A4.

I count six sheets of paper, insert them into the top of the machine. There is noise.

'You don't have to wear a suit, by the way.'

I look down at the internet suit. It does not fit.

I look at the documents.

The man walks away.

This room is noisy. Machines, wheels, shouting. Men, women who look like men. Stationery, metal shelves. The workers throw envelopes into boxes, bags. They wear trainers, T-shirt, jeans.

I do not want to destroy the documents. The documents have meaning. The documents are not like me.

£969.8m

£200m

5.8%

£17,312.7m

£16,312.1m
£200.0m
£13,044.3m
£15,572.3m
£749.8m
4.5%
£200m
£2,568.4m
13.5%

At half past nine, I insert documents into the machine.

At ten, I insert documents into the machine.

Ten thirty, I insert documents into the machine.

I remove my tie, stuff it into my pocket.

Every five minutes, I remove the lid, empty the shredded paper into a black dustbin bag. A nest for Owl.

Where is the toilet?

A man brings boxes. Inside the boxes, paper, documents.

I look at the documents. Do not read the documents. The documents were printed on a laser printer. Or, they are photocopies of documents printed on a laser printer.

At eleven, I put on my tie, walk out of the post room. I do not want to work in the post room. I do not want to shred the documents.

Corridors, the lift. Plants in metal pots. Ceiling tiles.

Above my head, several floors up, Edward.

I sit in the canteen. It is not lunchtime. The canteen is empty. Then, the canteen is not empty. Two men. The men sit near me.

'It's even more spectacular on the inside,' one of the men says. 'The second tallest building in the City.'

'I hope there's a lift.'

'There's several lifts.' The man sips his coffee. 'They move at six metres per second.'

'Is that fast?'

The man nods his head. 'It is also environmentally friendly.'

'The lift or the building?'

The man does not say.

The men wear grey suits, grey socks.

On the table, white dust.

On the table, a newspaper.

Expense and mortality assumptions used in the calculation were best estimates based on investigations carried out during 2005.

I read this.

I stand, walk out of the canteen, through the foyer, out into the street.

# 42

I open Edward's briefcase. I do not know the combination. I do not need the combination. Edward's briefcase is not locked.

Do you trust me, Edward?

Four-bedroomed house in Holland Park. Balconies, bathrooms. Paintings, antiques. Edward is in the kitchen, making coffee. Edward's study is painted lime green, the colour of Ad's fridge.

Edward lives here with his wife, Alicia. For a woman of eighty-eight, Alicia is beautiful.

Edward's briefcase contains documents. I take out one of the documents.

I will hear Edward's shoes on the stairs. Edward will climb the stairs slowly. Do not spill coffee on your bespoke suit.

Alicia is in the back garden. Alicia wears a white dress, brown sandals. If I stand, I can see her. Between fingers, the stalk.

With hands like fallen leaves, Alicia holds the flower.

I close Edward's briefcase. In my pocket, the document, folded.

Edward comes in. Edward holds two cups of coffee.

'Come through here,' Edward says.

I follow Edward.

'This is where Alicia works.'

The walls are lined with bookshelves. The books are old. Yes, like Alicia. Edward tells me this. Alicia inherited the books.

The mirror is framed, ornate.

'This is the computer,' Edward says.

I know that.

It is not a penguin.

It is not a trombone.

It is a computer.

Edward boots up the computer, logs on to Windows XP. The computer is slow. Edward stirs his coffee. The screen changes colour. Icons appear, one by one, slow.

'It's probably a virus,' Edward says.

I ask Edward why he thinks this. Edward says that he does not know.

Alicia has a special chair, for her back. I sit in the special chair, at the computer.

I click the icon for the hard drive and click properties. I click the tools tab, run Disk Defragmenter and request a report. The report tells me that the drive is 49% fragmented.

Edward stirs his coffee.

While the drive defragments, I search the internet for free anti-virus and anti-spyware software. I download the software and install it on the computer.

This, while Edward drinks coffee, makes a phone call, uses the loo.

Edward could have done this himself. Edward does not

need me to do this.

Edward kicks off his shoes.

Edward has biscuits. There is nothing like a biscuit.

Alicia comes in from the garden. I hear the sandals on the wooden stairs. On the study carpet, Alicia's sandals are silent.

'Alicia, say hello to Michael.'

In the doorway, Alicia.

Alicia holds out her hand. I hold the hand, do not move it. 'You were at my party with the young girl, Rebecca.'

I nod. Rebecca is my girlfriend.

'Michael has found three viruses,' Edward says.

'Is that right?'

The software found the viruses. I did not find the viruses. I tell Alicia that I need the toilet.

Alicia smiles.

In the bathroom, I remove my trainers, jeans, T-shirt, underpants, socks. I stand in front of the mirror. The mirror is huge, ornate. Everything in Edward and Alicia's house is huge. I am not huge, not on any level.

I find the back pocket of my jeans and remove the document. The document is folded into quarters. I unfold the document.

Investment Funds Management.

Authorised Investment Funds.

Asia Pacific Eq Ret Acc.

Asia Pacific Eq Ret Inc.

Div Target Ret Ret Acc.

Equity High Inc Ret Acc.

Euro Disc Ret Acc.

Euro Ethical Ret Acc.

I read, aloud. I stand in front of the mirror and read the document. I fail to understand.

I fold the document into quarters, place it in the back pocket of my jeans, dress, flush the toilet and return to Alicia's study.

Edward and Alicia are sitting on the bed, holding hands.

I sit on the chair.

I do not look at Edward and Alicia.

# 43

I watched Baby Girl check her emails. This happened yesterday. Baby typed her email address, her password. The password appeared as asterisks. There were six.

Baby Girl typed with two fingers. The fingers moved quickly, too quickly. Baby typed with her right hand, covered the hand with her left hand.

Baby went to the toilet. I heard her lift the seat.

Patsy and Owl kept watch at the door, the door that leads to the hall.

I opened the key logger folder and opened the log file. I scrolled to the end of the document. The file contains the date, the time, 11.34, and a series of letters. These are the letters Baby typed with her fingers. The six letters of Baby Girl's password are the six letters that follow the email address. The letters are y, e, l, p, e, r.

'She's on the toilet,' Patsy said. 'I just heard a tinkle.'

Yelper is the name of Baby Girl's toy dog.

I logged into Baby Girl's email account. I found an email from Milo. I did not read the email. I clicked reply, typed an email to Milo.

I hate you.

I hate you.

'She's wiping,' Patsy said.

I logged out of Baby Girl's email account, closed the laptop. This happened yesterday.

Today, Baby Girl and Milo argue. This happens at Ad's flat.

Milo asks Baby Girl about the email. Baby says she does not know. Milo says that she does know.

'You sent it. You said you hate me. Why?'

'I didn't.'

'You did. Why?'

'I didn't. I don't know.'

Baby Girl cries. Puts her shoes on. The buckles shine. Wet with tears, Baby walks out into the street.

I follow.

Behind Baby, my footsteps.

I put my arm around Baby Girl. I feel her tears on my cheek. This is where I want to feel the tears. Here, in this street, with the wind and the moving leaves.

# 44

I open the front door.

Alanna.

I met Alanna at the Red Lion in Ealing, the day after we moved in to Edward's flat. Patsy and Owl met her, too.

Owl did not approve. Owl is old fashioned, a gentleman.

Alanna looks at me, laughs. 'You look like a robot,' Alanna says.

I am wearing the internet suit. I look like a robot, an invader.

Alanna is here to see Baby Girl.

Edward asked the tailor how long the bespoke suit will take to make. 'Usually a couple of months. It depends on the time of year. Autumn is a quiet time. It may be possible to finish it in two to three weeks.'

At the front door, Alanna laughs at my trainers. A cardboard suit, with trainers.

Why did Edward buy me a bespoke suit? Edward bought me the suit in payment. The suit is my salary. This is a transaction, a deal. It is business.

At the front door, Alanna asks me if Baby Girl is here.

Yes. Come through.

Baby Girl and Alanna sit on the bed. Alanna puts her hair

in bunches, like Baby Girl. The two girls want to look the same. There is comfort in this. Baby hands Alanna two hair clips. Alanna reaches up, puts them in.

I do not look like Alanna or Baby Girl.

Do I look like Edward?

Baby Girl whispers in Alanna's ear. Alanna laughs.

Baby and Alanna remove shoes and socks, compare toes. Which are more bendy?

In Baby's hand, the toy dog, Yelper. She found him under my pillow. Last night, I could not sleep. I put Yelper under my pillow and slept.

I sit on the edge of the bed. Spacious studio in the City. I could stand at the kitchen sink, sit on the toilet, run a bath.

Baby and Alanna practise kissing. They kiss their hands, each other's hands. They kiss each other on the lips.

Do I look like Patsy? Or Owl?

Milo? Ad?

I watch Baby Girl and Alanna kiss. I watch, then look away. I look at my knees in the suit. Tonight, I will kiss Patsy. I will practise on the back of my hand. No one will see.

Alanna asks Baby Girl if she likes my suit.

'I hate suits,' Alanna says.

'I like Edward's suit,' Baby Girl says.

In this room, you can hear the fridge buzz. You hear this at night. The sound buzzes into your head. Patsy said that the fridge is powered by bees.

Alanna asks Baby about Edward. Who is he? And where did you two meet?

'We haven't done it,' Baby Girl says. 'I let him finger me though.'

I want to ask Baby why she likes Edward.

Why?

You hate your father?

You love your father?

Because it's wrong?

You find older men attractive?

Edward is rich?

He wears a bespoke suit?

Older men are more experienced?

He's married?

It is not my place to ask. This is none of my business.

I walk around the flat. I open, close the fridge door. From the bathroom, I hear the voices of two girls. I look at my face in the mirror. I straighten my tie. In the kitchen, I unfold the newspaper. I find words, figures. I copy these into the back of the notebook.

FTSE

Wed 15:15

3410.30

12.62

down

0.37

down

15.84

down

0.92

down

In the kitchen, I ask Baby Girl why she likes Edward.

'He's nice,' Baby Girl says.

# 45

Alanna wants to stay the night.

'There's no room,' Patsy says. 'There's only room for three humans and an owl.'

The double bed is for Patsy, me. Owl sleeps in Patsy's arms. Under the bed, Baby's mattress. We pull the mattress out, spread the sheet, the duvet.

'We can sleep on this,' Alanna says. 'It might fit two.'

Baby Girl shakes her head.

'We can try.'

Patsy changes into her nightie, gets into bed.

I strip to my underpants, climb into bed beside Patsy.

On the single mattress, Baby Girl and Alanna fight for the single duvet.

The clock ticks.

At the window, behind the curtains, darkness, lights.

Patsy lies with her back to me, Owl tucked into her tummy. Patsy protects him. Patsy is his nest, his parent.

Patsy is wearing a silk nightie. The material feels clingy, soft. Patsy's bottom is big and warm. This makes me feel safe. Patsy protects me. Patsy is my nest, my parent.

The clock ticks.

I hold Patsy, listen to her breathing. I listen as Patsy falls asleep.

The duvet moves, and Baby Girl is here.

In the dark, eyes shine.

I move my arm from under the duvet and place my hand on the shape of Baby Girl's body. Baby does not move away. The world does not fall apart.

'Dear oh dear, how sad I feel today. There is no rhyme nor reason to any of it.'

Patsy

# 46

Alicia did not know what to cook. What do young men eat?

I am twenty-two. Rebecca is nineteen. Edward told Alicia these ages. The ages are false.

'I've made a selection,' Alicia says. 'Anything we don't eat we can freeze.'

'You can't freeze spaghetti,' Edward says.

Alicia laughs. 'Alicia can freeze anything,' Alicia says.

This is Edward's home in Holland Park. Balconies, bathrooms, pillars.

This is the dining room.

The table is huge, antique. The table is spread with a tablecloth. On the tablecloth, plates. On the plates, food.

Alicia describes the food. Spaghetti, roasted red mullet, chillies, black olives. The herbs are thyme. Penne pasta, dried porcini mushrooms, tomato, garlic. The herbs are parsley. Linguine, crab. Yes, this is crab meat. This is fennel. Roast wild duck. There are vegetables in white bowls.

Always use fresh herbs, Alicia says.

Baby Girl folds her hands in her lap. The fingers hold Yelper. 'Can I have the tomato pasta?' Baby Girl says.

Alicia holds the ladle, Baby's plate. Returns the plate to the table.

For Edward and Alicia, duck. Edward carves the duck. Alicia uses her fingers. Alicia lays the sliced duck on the plate. 'Help yourself to vegetables,' Alicia says.

I have spaghetti and mullet.

What is mullet?

Alicia tells me that mullet is fish. It's fresh.

Edward explains that the mullet is a ray-finned fish found in tropical waters.

Baby Girl says that a mullet is a hairstyle. Milo had this hairstyle when they met. She told him to get it cut, and he did.

'Who is Milo?' Alicia says.

'Rebecca's previous boyfriend,' Edward says, 'before Michael.'

Baby looks at me, nods, laughs.

I hold Baby's hand.

When we are together, when Alicia is here, Baby Girl is my girlfriend. Not Milo's. Not Edward's. Mine.

Alicia walks into the kitchen.

In my pocket, five hundred pounds. This is business, a deal. Edward hired me to do this.

Edward whispers into my ear. 'Kiss Baby.'

I kiss Baby Girl on the cheek.

'No. The lips.'

I kiss Baby Girl on the lips. Baby Girl does not move away.

'Tongues,' Edward whispers.

I kiss Baby Girl with my tongue. When Alicia comes in, I stop.

We eat. There is conversation.

Alicia and Edward stand, collect plates.

Alicia asks me and Rebecca how we met.

I look at Rebecca. Um.

I tell Alicia that I met Baby Girl last summer, at the funfair. No, on the beach. We went to the funfair together. The story moves as I invent it. We went on rides.

'I love funfairs,' Baby says.

Alicia thanks me for fixing her computer. 'It no longer eats my important files.'

Edward massages Baby's shoulders. He does this, and looks at Alicia, at her face.

Alicia frowns.

Alicia tips salt over her shoulder.

On the carpet, behind Alicia, salt.

# 47

I open the front door.

Not Alanna.

Not Patsy, back with tinned vole for Owl.

The visitor is Milo. He wants to see Baby Girl. 'Is she home?'

Yes.

'Will you get her?'

No.

'Can I come in?'

No.

Milo comes in, pushes past. Behind Milo, Ad.

In the hallway, me, Baby Girl. Baby in pink flip-flops, towel. Baby Girl was painting her toenails. Two toenails have been painted. Lime green, the colour of Ad's fridge.

In Baby's hand, the bottle of nail polish.

It is afternoon.

Baby Girl turns, walks into the main room. I follow. Then Milo, Ad.

Milo looks around the flat. 'Is this your place?'

Baby points at me. 'And him.'

'You two are shacked up?'

'Yes, with Patsy.'

'The woman with the big arse?'

Baby Girl nods.

Ad looks at the Smeg fridge. The fridge is like Ad's fridge. The flat is decorated like Ad's flat. This flat is smaller, could fit inside Ad's bathroom.

Milo points at Baby Girl's toes, her toenails. Two lime green, eight skin pink. 'Are you painting your toes again?'

Baby looks at her toes, nods.

'You're always painting your nails,' Milo says.

Ad opens the fridge, looks inside. 'You've got the same fridge as me. Though yours has got food in.'

Milo laughs.

'And the same kettle. And the exact same toaster.'

'I didn't choose them.'

'Then who did?'

Baby Girl looks at me.

I tell Ad and Milo that the products belong to the landlord.

Ad opens, closes cupboards. 'It just seems a bit of a coincidence you would have the exact same stuff.'

I nod. Yes.

Ad looks out of the window.

Milo sits on the bed.

Baby Girl tells Milo not to sit on the bed. 'You can't sit on my bed if you dumped me.'

'Rebecca, you were the one who ended it, not me. You emailed me and told me you hate me.'

Baby Girl shakes her head.

Milo lifts his right leg, rests it across his left leg. Picks dry leaves from the tread of his trainer. Milo drops the leaves onto the bed.

Baby Girl reaches for my hand. We hold hands.

Milo shakes his head, unhappy.

Ad steps into the hall, pulls Milo by the corner of his T-shirt. Alienation, boredom, despair. These are feelings we all experience from time to time.

'This is disabled,' Milo says.

The front door slams.

We sit together on the bed. Baby's hand in my hand, her hand held tight. This, until the key turns in the lock, and Patsy is here with Owl.

Baby Girl needs the toilet. She has been drinking Coke. The can moved across the floor. This, when Ad kicked it.

Baby lifts the toilet seat. We hear the sound.

Patsy looks at the leaves. Dry, broken, brown.

I sit on the bed with Patsy. I ask Patsy if the leaves belong to Owl.

'Yes. He collects them.'

Patsy fetches tissues from the kitchen worktop. Wraps the leaves in tissues. Opens the wooden trunk. Moves clothes from the corner, places the tissues in the corner, beneath clothes. Closes the wooden lid.

The leaves will be safe here.

# 48

'Two weeks before,' the man says, 'you buy your alcohol, your wine and mixers.'

Baby Girl giggles.

The man wears a salmon coloured shirt with black buttons.

The man wags his finger at the woman.

'One week before is when you buy your groceries. But not the fresh produce. That's very important.'

This is Alicia and Edward's party. But where is Alicia, where is Edward?

Behind the bar, staff polish glasses.

'Three days before, clean the main part of the house.'

'Why three days?'

'Any longer and you'll need to clean it again. Two days before, prepare your poultry.'

The bar is called Icon. I do not know why the bar is called this.

Edward paid me to be here. In my pocket, the money.

The man and the woman hold drinks. I ask Baby Girl what she would like to drink.

'Vodka and orange,' Baby says, 'with ice.'

People arrive.

We stand by the bar, hold hands.

The man in the salmon coloured shirt is telling the woman how to organise a cocktail party. 'You will need ice. Oh, and you will need flowers. Order these a week in advance, to arrive the day before the party.'

I order the drinks. Vodka and orange for Baby Girl, bottle of lager for me. Lager is artificially carbonated.

Edward walks in, with Alicia. On Alicia's cheek, glitter. Edward's tie is pale blue.

On Baby Girl's cheek, glitter.

More people arrive. Edward and Alicia stand by the door, hug people, shake hands, say hello. Men kiss Alicia on the cheek.

I kiss Baby Girl's cheek.

In make-up, Baby looks eighteen, nineteen. Baby Girl is fifteen, a child.

I let go of Baby's hand.

We stand at the bar and watch people arrive, shake hands, kiss, say hello.

'It manages to be both confused and confusing,' a man says.

This is confusing.

I watch Edward walk up to the bar.

Edward orders drinks. Wine, a cocktail. The cocktail is for Alicia. Edward straightens his tie. Edward's tie is pale blue.

The barman mixes the cocktail. Cognac, apricot brandy, lemon juice, garlic, ice, ginger beer. I look at the bottles. The barman shakes the cocktail shaker. Pours the liquid into the glass. Slice of lime. Puts the glass on the bar.

Edward winks at me.

Edward carries the cocktail to Alicia. Sips his wine.

I look at the bottle of lager in my hand.

People talk to me and Baby Girl. The people ask us questions. How do you know Edward, Alicia? How did the two of you meet?

Here, a man who fancies Baby Girl. The man stands in front of me, does not look at me. The man looks, smiles at Baby Girl. 'Write down your phone number. I may call you sometime.'

'I don't think my boyfriend would like that.'

'Who is your boyfriend?'

Baby Girl points at me.

Oh.

The man walks away.

Baby Girl laughs, squeezes my hand.

Edward hands me a drink. I look at the drink. The drink is red. There is a slice of lime on the side of the glass. Edward smiles, walks away.

'He didn't get me one,' Baby Girl says.

I get Baby Girl a drink. The drink is a cocktail. I ask the barman for a cocktail. The barman shows me a list. I choose a cocktail from the list. I tell the barman the name of the cocktail. The barman mixes the cocktail. I carry the cocktail to Baby Girl.

Baby looks at the drink, laughs.

I drink my drink. In my drink, a piece of paper. I take the piece of paper from my drink. The glass is half empty. Baby's glass is half full. I unfold the piece of paper, read.

Follow me to the gents. Smudged, the words say this.

I look at Edward. He nods, walks.

I follow Edward through the crowd, through a door.

Edward leans against the sink. 'Michael, Alicia suspects.'

I don't say anything.

'My relationship with Baby Girl. What shall I do?'

I shrug. I don't know.

I want you to find me a job. Not in the post room. In an office. I want you to teach me about futures, money, business.

%

52 wk-h

52 wk-l

6613.30

17.60

down

0.27

down

6732.40 5681.70

Equity groups.

Shares, bonds, stocks.

'Michael, I know you're not one to speak your mind but I am asking you what I should do about my relationship with Baby Girl. Should I stop seeing her?'

I nod.

'You think I should terminate my relationship with Baby Girl.'

I nod.

Edward looks at himself in the mirror, straightens his tie, wets his hair. Checks the lines under his eyes, tries to smooth them. Edward adjusts cufflinks. Walks to the door. Turns, looks at me. 'Tell Baby Girl I do not want to see her. Remove her from the party, then tell her.'

I watch the door open, close.

# 49

The pub is called the Fox. We walked from Soho. Held hands, walked.

Baby Girl did not want to leave the party. Baby wanted to say goodbye to Edward.

We sit, drink.

The barman did not believe that Baby Girl is eighteen. Don't try me, the barman said.

Lager. Orange juice.

Yesterday Patsy told me not to look at Baby Girl. Avert your gaze, Patsy said. I told Patsy that I was not looking at Baby Girl.

I was looking at the air in front of her face.

I was counting specks of dust.

I was not looking at anything. My eyes were closed.

I was looking at my reflection in Baby Girl's eyes.

I was looking at Baby, but I was thinking about you.

Thoughts, concepts inserted into Patsy's head.

The pub is busy, rowdy.

I tell Baby that Edward does not want to see her any more.

'Why?'

'Because of Alicia,' I say. 'Edward is a married man.'

'But I love him.'

You don't love Edward. You love Milo, Yelper.

Or, me.

'Why doesn't he want to see me?'

'He thinks Alicia suspects something.'

'But Michael, why?'

'I don't know.'

Baby starts to cry. I did not expect this.

Baby Girl cries for one minute. The clock is above the bar. Baby stops crying, wipes her eyes.

I told Patsy that I have no interest in Baby Girl. Patsy believed this. In Patsy's world, everything is true.

I gulp some of my lager.

Baby Girl looks into her orange juice for answers. There are no answers. The liquid is opaque.

# 50

Patsy pushes the trolley. In the front basket, Owl. Owl is the driver.

I tell Patsy that we should spend Edward's money. We should stock up. At the checkout, Patsy asks me why.

Why should we spend Edward's money?

Why should we stock up?

I tell Patsy about the party, about Edward and Baby. Edward put a note in my drink.

'What party? Why didn't you invite me?'

'You didn't want to come.'

Patsy accepts this. In Patsy's world, everything is true.

'Edward and Baby Girl broke up.'

Patsy opens her mouth to speak, does not speak.

People move forward. I start to lift tins onto the conveyor belt.

'You split them up because you want to go out with Baby.'

I shake my head. No.

'Then why did you split them up?'

'I didn't split them up. Edward was worried about Alicia.'

'Oh.'

I tell Patsy to help with the tins.

Patsy looks at the tins.

Patsy moves a tin onto the conveyor belt.

We pay, pile the tins into carrier bags, leave.

Patsy carries the three bags. This is her idea. When I try to take one of the bags, Patsy does not let me. Patsy is a carthorse. Patsy is a pit pony. This is how Patsy describes herself.

Owl wants to ride in one of the carrier bags. Well, someone has to guard the tins. Perhaps the tins contain owl food. Perhaps the tins contain vole. There is a jar of mice.

At the bus stop, Patsy puts the three carrier bags on the pavement.

Owl rolls out of his bag onto the pavement. Patsy does not see this. I do not tell her. In a moment, Patsy will see him on the kerb, pick him up, dust his tummy, hold him.

I hold Patsy's hand and tell Patsy what will happen. We are to be made redundant. Edward does not need us. Edward will tell us to move out.

Patsy puts my hand into her pocket. Her hand holds my hand. Patsy's hand is bigger than my hand. I cannot remove my hand from Patsy's pocket.

## 51

Patsy wants an ice lolly.

Before Patsy went into the newsagent, I asked her why she wants an ice lolly. It is cold today. Patsy said that the lolly will freeze her insides and she will not be able to feel anything. I took her hand and asked her what she does not want to feel. Patsy looked at Baby, at me. Patsy said that she did not want to feel sad. Then Patsy went into the newsagent.

Through the window, I can see Patsy. I watch as she lifts the lid of the freezer.

Baby Girl coughs.

I stand with Baby Girl on the kerb. We watch the cars. The cars make a lot of noise.

Patsy comes out of the shop and unwraps her ice lolly.

'Let's go back to the flat,' Baby Girl says.

I hold Patsy's hand. Her other hand holds the lolly, which is red.

Baby Girl stops to sort out her shoe.

I tell Patsy to stop, and she stops.

Patsy asks me about the flat. Do we have to leave the flat?

Yes, I say. We have to leave the flat. But not today.

'Owl loves that flat,' Patsy says.

We are near Bethnal Green or Old Street.

Baby Girl runs to catch up. She is barefoot. I can see the shoes on the kerb. 'The heel broke,' Baby Girl says.

'Your feet will get dirty,' Patsy says.

Patsy offers Baby Girl some of her ice lolly. Baby Girl smiles and bites the lolly. Some falls off. Baby catches the ice and ice cream in her hand. Puts it into her mouth.

We walk.

'I don't care about my feet,' Baby Girl says.

Patsy asks Baby Girl if she cares about Edward.

Baby Girl shrugs.

We cross the road at the zebra crossing.

'I wanted the one with yellow ice cream in the middle,' Patsy says.

'They stopped making them,' Baby Girl says. 'Why does everything have to end?'

# 52

Edward wanted to meet in the park. I do not know why Edward wanted to do this.

The park is in the City, near Edward's office.

I look at the time on my mobile. Edward is late.

I look at the newspaper.

Prison sentences could be given to those who deliberately misuse personal data.

The park is circular, surrounded by buildings, offices. I do not work in an office. Edward works in an office, but not one of these offices. Edward's building shimmers, at night, during the day.

There is a man here. The man is not Edward. The man is the opposite of Edward. I watch the man sort through the rubbish in the litter bin. The man is homeless, a tramp. The man holds a radio, loud, detuned. No music, only fuzz. The man sorts through the rubbish. Pulls something out, looks at it, drops it back in.

Edward arrives. I watch Edward walk towards me.

Edward sits with me on the bench.

We face wilted flowers.

'I cannot live without her,' Edward says.

Who?

Baby Girl? Alicia?

'Tell Baby Girl I want her back. Tell her to meet me tonight, at a bar in Soho, the bar we went to the other night. I forget the name.'

'Icon.'

'Was it called that?'

Beside Edward on the bench, I nod.

The tramp stands near us. In his arms, the radio. Fuzz sounds from the radio. The man does not tune it in. There is something wrong with the radio. Or, there is something wrong with the man.

'What a dreadful name for a bar. Why is it called Icon?'

I do not know.

'Bars used to have interesting names. These days it's always the name of an animal or something abstract. Michael, when did the world get so pretentious?'

I tell Edward I do not know.

'Not there,' Edward says. 'A restaurant. Yes.'

On the grass, leaves, bread. Birds pick the bread from the leaves. Toss, peck.

Edward looks at the man. 'If Alicia left me I'd end up like him.'

Alicia is old. There is limited time. I do not say this.

The tramp reaches into the bottom of the bin. For this, he puts down the radio. Pulls out a Coke can, shakes it, drops it back into the bin.

We watch the man take things from the bin, examine them, drop them back in.

Edward is wearing a bespoke suit. Blue, checked. Edward loosens his tie. The tie is red with grey stripes.

The tramp wears trousers of no colour, a coat without

colour. The clothes have no shape, no meaning. The tramp takes a carton from the bin.

Edward looks at me and says, 'Michael, do you know what an albatross is?'

I nod. I do know this.

'An albatross is a type of bird. I want you to think about that for a moment.'

I do as instructed.

'Now think about my situation with Alicia and Baby Girl. Do you see my point?'

I nod.

I do not know what Edward is talking about.

High-street banks found guilty of discarding customer personal details including bank statements, cut-up credit cards and loan applications in unsecured bins outside their premises, the commissioner found.

Edward gets up, takes some coins from his pocket, offers the coins to the tramp.

The tramp looks at the coins as if they are shirt buttons. The tramp drops something into the bin, something he took from the bin, and walks off across the grass.

Edward looks at me, laughs, sits back down.

'If Alicia left me,' Edward says, jangling the coins in his pocket, 'I would end up like him. I would be his friend. We would sit and listen to the radio together and twiddle our thumbs.'

We can still hear the fuzz of the radio, quieter.

'I bet he hears that sound in his brain,' Edward says.

Edward puts his hand on my knee, looks at me, his face close to my face.

Do not touch me.

'Michael,' Edward says, 'it is imperative that Alicia does not find out about my relationship with Baby Girl.'

'The fridge contents were auditioning for a puppet show, singing and dancing stinkily.'

Patsy

# 53

The front door is blocked by a wheelbarrow.

In the wheelbarrow, a photograph. Black and white, faded, curled. Patsy holds the photograph in her hands. The photograph shows people at a wedding. Top hat, tails. The bride and groom hold hands.

Patsy does not know who these people are.

Patsy's mother collects things.

The house is Patsy's mother's house in Kent.

The back door is blocked too, by a fridge. The fridge door is open, there is food. The cord tangled into the grass, the plug lost among nettles.

'She must have climbed in through the window,' Patsy says.

We walk around the outside of the house twice, step over things. The windows are painted shut, the paint coating the wood, the glass. A layer peels, yellow as butter.

Patsy has not seen her mother for years.

'How did she get the wheelbarrow against the door?'

Patsy does not know.

Patsy's mother is frail, the size of Patsy's finger.

What is wrong with that wheel? The wheelbarrow is stuck, the wheel locked in concrete. The wheelbarrow was left here when the concrete set.

'She upset the builders,' Patsy says. 'Shouted out of the window.'

In the apple tree, birds sing, amused.

I reach over the wheelbarrow, ring the bell.

We step back, look up at the house, the roof. Arms folded, we wait.

'She could be dead,' Patsy says.

Inside this house, Patsy's mother lies dead.

A miniature lady of eighty-five. Her head in a bag of knitting. Her body buried in photographs, pictures.

Patsy never cared much for her mother.

How do we get in?

Inside this house, a tiny woman breathes into a paper bag. Keels over, dead.

Patsy's mother, small as salt.

Patsy has the arms of a shire horse. This is her description. With effort, she can heave the wheelbarrow across the lawn. I hold Patsy's bag, the photograph. Patsy wrenches the wheelbarrow from the ground. Bolts pop out, rattle onto concrete.

Inside the house, the woman spills her tea.

Patsy has a key, kept it for years. She left home aged twelve. The door opens, we have to push it. Leaflets, bills. Mrs Reaner, 4 Nith Street, Kent. Here's one for Patsy. Patricia J Reaner.

Patsy's mother is not here.

There is a knitting bag, contains knitting.

Buttons dance on the silver tray. Patsy moves them with her finger. Eyes for toys never made.

Patsy's mother crocheted this cardigan, the cushion

covers, the tea cosy in the kitchen. The courgette bag, the only one of its kind in the world.

When Patsy was a girl, her mother knitted her a hat.

Patsy's mother did not make Owl. Patsy's mother would have stuffed him with garlic cloves, torn playing cards, cotton reels, pins.

# 54

Patsy cannot locate her mother.

Patsy made telephone calls from the payphone. In the pub, here. This is unusual. Like me, Patsy does not use the telephone.

Sitting beside Patsy, I read the newspaper.

Patsy made enquiries. Telephoned, wrote letters. Patsy sent a postcard. Siblings argued. Patsy replaced the handset, turned to me at the bar.

'There's another room,' Patsy tells me. 'I forgot.'

Here, girls talk, joke. What is your pornstar name?

First pet's name plus first street you lived in.

Corky Cross.

Sassy Pleasant.

Hawk Meadowland.

Sanford Gay Court.

I am sitting on a stool. Knees bent, trainers grip the wood.

Patsy does not have a stool. Patsy is standing at the bar, her hand on the payphone.

In Patsy's bag, our owl, Owl.

A girl passes a carrier bag over the bar to a girl with curly hair. This girl works here. The girls are colleagues, friends.

'The door is behind the mirror,' Patsy explains.

The room contains objects. Patsy's mother hoards things. Broken things, thrown-away things. Things you do not want. Things you do want. There are items Patsy's mother tucked under her coat.

Patsy's mother is clinically insane.

With hair like copper coins, the girl opens the bag. Inside, a birthday card. A man takes a pen from the till. Remove the cap, write it down. They sign, make comments, remarks. The name written on the envelope. Lick, seal.

Favourite soft drink or snack plus mother's maiden name.

Liquorice Aston.

Brandy Snaps Herbert.

Snickers Huntington.

Pepsi Worth.

Patsy's mother is a thief.

'I hid there as a little girl,' Patsy says. 'I stayed in that room for one week.'

'Why?'

'I wanted to feel safe.'

'What about your bedroom?'

'Mum spoilt my bedroom.'

Patsy, with biscuits.

Patsy curled beneath blankets.

Patsy, her eyes red, hid from shouting.

'I had a frightful crush on a boy who cycled past our house. I only fancied him when his cheeks flushed from panting up hills.'

Patsy

# 55

The address is in East London, Hackney. The address is written on a piece of paper. Baby Girl wrote the address on the piece of paper. Remove the cap, write it down. The voice on the telephone gave directions. Baby Girl drew a map.

Baby says that the artist will paint her portrait. This may take some time. Baby Girl explains this. Painting a portrait is an art, Michael. It is not like taking a photograph.

Yes. Yes.

Patsy wants to come with us.

I tell Patsy that she has to stay and look after Owl.

Oh but Owl wants to come too.

No. Owl will get paint on his feathers. Owl is a bird of distinction. Birds of distinction do not inhale paint fumes. Knitted birds and paint do not mix.

Patsy says she will stay and look after Owl.

I watch Patsy cuddle Owl.

I close the front door behind me and follow Baby Girl into the street.

On the bus, we talk about art. The bus stops, starts. Baby Girl tells me about an art book she looked at in a shop.

We walk from the bus stop to the studio. Baby Girl shows me the piece of paper, the map.

The studio is in a tatty Victorian warehouse just off Hackney Road. We look at the building. Broken windows, clogged drains.

'It might be nice inside,' Baby Girl says.

By the wall, parked cars.

The door is locked. No doorbell, no letterbox. We bang on the door with our fists. Baby Girl takes her phone from her pocket to call the artist. Before Baby Girl can find the artist's number, the door opens.

A girl holds the door open, invites us inside.

We go inside.

Tight denim skirt, denim shirt, white polka-dot shoes.

We follow the girl up the spiral metal staircase to a huge white room. The floorboards are spattered with paint. The paint is in many colours. Reds, blues, greens. White, black. The girl leads us across the room to a door. Behind the door, voices. The girl opens the door.

Inside the room, the artist. I recognise the artist from the cocktail party.

There are girls here.

The girls are sitting around a wooden table, drinking fizzy drinks from cans. One girl has a bottle of Coke.

I am not wearing my bespoke suit. The suit would get paint on it. The girls would like the bespoke suit. This is my internet suit. I do not care if I get paint on the internet suit.

The girls do not look at my internet suit. The suit has no value, no meaning.

There are tins of paint.

The artist kisses Baby Girl on the cheek. The artist leans against the wall.

The girl with the polka-dot shoes is the artist's assistant.

The artist tells us this. The assistant's name is Teresa. Hello, Teresa. We watch Teresa hang our coats on a hook. Other coats belong to the girls.

Each girl is barefoot.

The artist is dressed in baggy jeans, red jumper.

The artist's name is Daniel Lament.

We hear the sound of a toilet flushing. A door opens. A girl comes out, closes the door.

'I almost came to rescue you,' Daniel says.

The girl smiles, nods, does not laugh.

'Now,' Daniel says. Daniel closes the door, looks again at the girl who used the toilet. 'Anne, did I not ask you to remove your shoes and socks?'

Anne pulls out a chair, lifts her foot onto the chair. Anne tugs her shoelaces, pulls the trainer from her foot.

Laughter from girls.

'I love those socks,' Daniel says.

The socks have separate toes, each toe a different colour. The socks are like knitted gloves. Blue, purple, orange, green. The big toe is yellow. The rest of the sock is grey.

Daniel watches the girl remove her other trainer.

'And the socks, please.'

The girl sits on the chair, folds her arms. The girl does not remove her socks.

'This is foot painting,' Daniel tells the girl. 'You cannot paint with your feet if you're wearing socks.'

'You should have said on the phone,' the girl says.

Daniel looks at his assistant.

Teresa shrugs.

'I don't like people looking at my feet.'

Daniel asks the girl why she does not like people to see

her feet. 'Are your feet shy, Anne?'

Anne does not answer. Removes her socks, rolls them up, stuffs them into her shoes.

Anne sits on a chair.

Daniel looks at the girl's feet. 'They look fine to me.'

'I've got long toes,' Anne says.

One of the girls laughs.

Baby Girl leans towards me. 'I might go back to the flat.'

The artist hears this. 'If anyone wants to back out, that's fine. Remember however that you are being paid.'

Baby Girl puts her hand up.

'Hello,' Daniel says.

'I'm wearing tights,' Baby Girl says.

'You can change in here.' The artist opens the toilet door.

A girl says, 'Will we get paint on our feet?'

The artist nods his head. Yes.

'You never said that. When you said foot painting I thought you wanted to paint a portrait of my feet.'

The artist shakes his head. No.

The artist opens the fridge door. Inside the fridge, not much. Daniel takes a plastic tub from the fridge. Daniel removes the lid. The tub is clear. Inside the tub, sandwiches, white bread. Daniel lifts one of the corners. Inside the sandwich, meat. The meat is sandwich ham. Daniel tells me this. I do not know why Daniel tells me this. Daniel asks me if I am going to watch him eat the sandwich.

No. I am not.

The room smells of sandwich ham, the toilet, paint.

We follow the artist back into the studio. The artist, the assistant, girls with bare feet. I count the girls. There are twenty-two girls. And Baby makes twenty-three.

With a white bread sandwich in his mouth, the artist opens a tin of paint.

The artist and the assistant walk to the far end of the studio. On the floor, along the longest wall, a long roll of paper. Daniel and the assistant unroll the long roll of paper. The girls step out of the way. In trainers, I step out of the way. The assistant places tins of paint on the corners.

The girl stands on the paper in bare feet. Some of the girls stand on the floorboards at the side.

The assistant pours paint into trays.

The artist instructs the girls to step into the paint. 'Spread your toes,' the artist says. 'Let the paint ooze.'

The artist tells the girls to step out of the trays and walk on the sheet of paper.

The girls do this.

'Now,' the artist says. 'Walk.'

The girls walk around on the sheet of paper.

Teresa brings a stereo from the other room, plugs it into a socket, presses buttons. Music. I do not recognise the music. It is chart, it is pop.

'Don't follow each other,' the artist says. 'Try to find your own path. No half steps. Each footprint should be distinct.'

The girls avoid eye contact. Some of the girls giggle, laugh.

Baby Girl looks at me, rolls her eyes.

Baby finds her own path.

Patsy would not do this. Patsy would not let people see her bare feet. Patsy says her feet are cloven hooves.

Owl would do this. The feathered fellow would show them all how it's done. A classically trained actor, Owl would tread the boards. Owl would fly above the sheet of paper, dry the paint with his wings. Daniel would pay for this service.

A girl falls.

The girl trips, falls.

A swear word. Begins with s, ends with t. Rhymes with it, hit. Also, mitt.

The girl rolls in the paint.

Daniel shouts at the girl.

In shoes, Daniel walks across the painting.

# 56

Here, Edward said. Take this.

The envelope contained two hundred pounds in cash.

Take Baby Girl to a restaurant. Treat her, Edward said. Tell her you can go anywhere you like. Tell her you can dress up.

'I don't want to go anywhere I like,' Baby Girl said.

When I told Patsy that she could not come to the restaurant, she cried. To stop the tears, I told Patsy that she could come to the restaurant. You are invited. Patsy dried her eyes on Owl.

'If Edward doesn't want to see me any more,' Baby Girl said, 'why did he give you money to take me out?'

Because, I told her. And then, I did not complete the sentence.

Patsy wanted to bring Owl.

Yes. You can bring Owl. But he must wear his bib.

We waited by the front door for Baby to use the toilet.

# 57

The restaurant is in Shoreditch. We walk to the restaurant together. We walk the streets together. Patsy, Baby Girl, me.

Baby Girl likes it round here. Baby Girl tells us this.

Baby would not dress up. Too sad about Edward.

I did dress up. Patsy dressed up, too. Owl picked the fluff from his tummy feathers.

Baby Girl swings her arms.

The restaurant is called Horse. I do not know why the restaurant is called this. The restaurant serves hamburgers. The meat is quality meat. The meat is not horse meat.

I am wearing my bespoke suit. Edward collected it from the tailors. It is not like the internet suit. That suit does not fit. The bespoke suit does fit.

This is not fast food. A sign tells us this.

In my pocket, the envelope.

The restaurant is expensive for a hamburger restaurant, but it is not an expensive restaurant. There will be a lot of change from Edward's two hundred pounds.

Our hamburgers are handmade on the premises, it says here. Passers by read the words in their head, or heads.

We use only natural fed, grass-reared beef.

I flip a coin. This, for no reason.

I tell Patsy and Baby Girl to wait outside.

I go inside.

Patsy cannot sit with us. Sit with Baby Girl, Edward said. Sit beside, not opposite. I do not know why Edward said this.

The restaurant is decorated in dark brown and dark red. The walls are dark brown. The tables are dark red. The restaurant is not busy. Not today.

I take the envelope out of my pocket, hold it in my hand.

The waiters wear black T-shirts, black jeans, black shoes.

I ask to speak to the manager. The waiter gets the manager. This, with raised eyebrows.

The manager wears white shirt, blue jeans, trainers.

I tell the manager about Patsy and Owl. I have to tell the manager that Owl is not a real Owl, that Owl is made of wool, that Owl is knitted, stuffed. This may not be true.

The manager looks at me like I am an idiot. I am not an idiot. This may not be true.

I hand the manager five twenty-pound notes. There will not be much change from Edward's two hundred pounds.

The manager speaks to one of the waiters. You'd better hear this.

I tell the manager that Patsy will sit alone, with Owl. I tell the waiter to pull the chair out for Owl. He will need a cushion. Owl is short. Owl is vertically challenged. The only way for Owl to achieve height is to fly.

Owl will not fly in the restaurant. Owl has dignity. Owl has class.

No need to switch off the ceiling fans.

Whatever Owl wants, Owl gets. It will involve vole.

The waiter laughs.

'We don't serve vole,' the manager says.

Improvise. Blood could be ketchup. Red wine and raw meat for guts.

'Sit her away from the window. I don't want her to be laughed at or pointed at.'

Do not laugh at Patsy. Do not humiliate her. Do not draw attention to her. Do not patronise her. Patsy will turn tables. If you upset her, Patsy will shout.

The manager scratches his chin.

In a corner, leather sofas, cushions. The waiter fetches a cushion.

Outside, Patsy and Baby Girl watch through the window. I instruct them to enter the restaurant. To do this, I gesture with my hand.

Patsy takes Owl out of her bag. Owl wears a bib. This looks smart.

The waiter shows Patsy and Owl to a table.

The waiter pulls out a chair for Owl. The waiter plumps up the cushion, positions it on Owl's chair.

Patsy plumps up Owl.

Owl, you need to lose weight. Any fatter and you won't be able to swoop. You will be the laughing stock of the barn.

Patsy sits in the chair opposite Owl.

Patsy looks at me. 'Aren't we all sitting together?'

I tell Patsy that I will sit in two places at once, using magic.

Patsy shakes her head. This does not make sense.

I tell Patsy that Owl needs to speak with her in private. Matters involving dead mice and so forth.

Ah. This does make sense.

The waiter leads me and Baby Girl to a table by the window. Through the glass, people, clouds. Shoreditch is populated by young people who wear fashionable clothes. I watch these people.

I am not wearing fashionable clothes. I am dressed in my bespoke suit.

The table is a table for four. I sit beside Baby Girl at the table. Baby Girl asks me why I am sitting beside, not opposite. I tell her that I cannot tell her. I tell Baby Girl that I have something to tell her. Yes, a message from Edward. But first, I have to check on Patsy.

I walk back to Patsy's table. I stand beside Patsy and wait for the waiter to take Patsy's order.

The waiter flicks through his notepad.

Patsy orders a bacon cheeseburger with ketchup, red onion and lettuce. And vole pizza for Owl.

'We don't actually serve pizza,' the waiter says.

I look at the waiter. I cough, clear my throat.

'We could rustle up a quick vole burger.'

Owl's eyes shine, bright as buttons.

I return to my seat.

We wait for the food to arrive.

I tell Baby the good news. I put my hand on her wrist and speak. 'I have a message from Edward,' I say. 'He wants to continue the relationship.'

Baby Girl smiles. She is happy.

We watch the waiters serve people. Young people in fashionable clothes. Two men in shirt, tie. Sitting alone, an old man.

From the far side of the restaurant, Patsy's posh voice, Owl's patronising squawk.

On Owl's bib, vole blood.

I stand, walk. I want the customers to see my bespoke suit. I work in the City, like Edward.

Through the window, Edward.

Hello, Edward.

Edward in jumper, jeans. Edward behind a parked car. Edward looks at me. No wave, no smile. Edward has brushed his hair.

Owl spits vole guts onto the floor.

Waiter, clean this.

I walk back to the table and sit beside Baby Girl.

The waiter brings Coke, lager, two glasses. The Coke is in a clear plastic bottle. The lager is in a green glass bottle. The waiter pours the drinks. We watch the waiter do this.

Behind the waiter, Edward.

Baby smiles.

I will sit with Patsy, Owl. Owl will sit on my lap. Do not dig your claws in.

Edward grabs my elbow. 'Stay. I want to talk with you both together.'

I sit with Baby Girl, our backs to the dark brown wall. Edward is sitting opposite. Edward rolls up his sleeves.

The waiter brings our burgers. For me, for Baby Girl.

Edward orders wine, salad.

Baby Girl picks up her burger. 'I need a fork,' Baby Girl says.

Edward snaps his fingers. Requests cutlery.

I watch Baby Girl bite her burger. On Baby's fingers, ketchup. The ketchup looks like blood.

I look at my burger.

The waiter brings knife, fork, wine.

I look at Edward, say nothing.

Edward folds his hands on the table, looks about him, tries to speak.

Then, Edward does speak.

'You and Patsy, Michael. The two of you offer a service. I require you to perform that service.'

I look at my burger.

'I want you to do something for me. If you do as I ask, you keep the flat. That is my payment to you. I will sign the flat over to your name. Yourself and Patsy. If you do this. This that I ask.'

I look at Edward.

'There is something Baby and I want to do, have wanted to do, and have not done. It will be done, and I want you and Patsy to be present.'

Baby Girl bites her bottom lip.

Edward tips his glass of wine. The wine looks like blood.

'Let's talk about this tomorrow. I have to get back. I have to meet Alicia.'

# 58

Baby Girl is making coffee. Baby Girl does not drink coffee. Baby drinks orange juice, Coke.

In the street, Patsy. I watch Patsy through the window. Patsy throws Owl up into the air. Owl swoops through the air. Owl is a homing owl. Owl lands on Patsy's head, her arm, the pavement.

Patsy in boots like old-fashioned kettles. Patsy in a cowboy shirt. Three petticoats make a pretty dress.

Baby turns, carries the cup of coffee to the bed. Baby Girl made this for herself. Baby is a coffee drinker, like Edward. Baby sits, sips.

I step away from the window.

Baby Girl takes her laptop from under the bed.

'This is the computer,' Baby Girl tells me.

I know that.

It is not a cream cake.

It is not a box of chocolates.

It is a computer.

Baby Girl opens the lid. The laptop boots up. Baby logs on to Windows XP. The laptop is slow. Baby stirs her coffee. The screen changes colour. Icons appear, one by one, slow.

'Has it got a virus?'

I shake my head, though I do not know this.

I sit on the edge of the bed, the laptop on my lap.

Baby Girl sips her coffee. 'I like a nice cup of coffee,' Baby Girl says.

I ask Baby Girl why she is drinking coffee.

'Edward and I had coffee together yesterday. He took me to a coffee shop in Soho.'

I click the icon for the hard drive and click properties. I click the tools tab, run Disk Defragmenter, request a report. The report tells me that the drive is 28% fragmented.

Baby Girl stirs her coffee.

On Baby's laptop, stickers. A horse, a cartoon star.

Baby tells me that the artist did not pay.

The girl slipped, fell. The painting was ruined. The artist was upset by this. Daniel slapped himself on the head, covered his eyes with his hands. Daniel Lament instructed us to leave. The girls would not leave. Not with paint on our feet, the girls said.

Teresa asked me to help.

Yes. I will help.

Get them cleaned up. Through here.

Teresa poured liquid into the bath. The liquid will remove the paint. Teresa is the name of the artist's assistant. Teresa turned the taps.

Water poured into the bath.

I watched the girls clean their feet. I helped steady the girls. The girls held on to my shoulders. My shoulders are not broad, but they can be held.

Paint from between the toes.

Paint from beneath toenails.

Paint in all the colours of the rainbow.

I think about this.

I download anti-virus software from the internet and install the software.

Baby Girl kicks off her sandals, shows paint that remains. 'It was funny when the girl fell over.'

I laugh. The laugh is not real.

When I laugh, people look at me like I invade.

When Patsy laughs, people look at her like they are afraid. Patsy laughs a lot. When Patsy laughs, Owl bounces in Patsy's lap.

Owl does not laugh. This is a sign of Owl's superiority.

When Baby Girl laughs, people laugh, smile.

Or, they die inside.

Baby wriggles her toes. I look at the toes. Under the toenails, paint. The paint is blue. Baby Girl chose blue paint. Pink is too obvious, Baby Girl said.

I hear the front door open, close.

Patsy walks into the room, looks at us sitting together on the bed, sits on the bed, on the other side of the bed. Patsy and Baby back to back, without words.

In the pocket of my jeans, the document. This taken from Edward's briefcase.

I stand.

In the kitchen, I pretend to tidy objects. The objects are tins, jars. I do this until Patsy and Baby Girl speak.

Baby shows Patsy something on the laptop. This will cheer you up, Baby Girl says. A screensaver. Daft pets.

The flat is small. This means that I am always near Baby Girl. And, I am always near Patsy.

I find my bespoke suit and carry it to the bathroom.

In the bathroom, I remove my jeans, T-shirt, socks,

underpants, and stand in front of the mirror. I unfold the document, read.

Glbl Inv European Opps Bd.

Glbl Inv European Opps Bd.

Insight Inv Asia Pacific Eq A Acc.

Insight Inv Asia Pacific Eq A Inc.

Insight Inv Asia Pacific Port Acc.

I do not understand what the words mean.

Div Target Ret Ret Acc.

Equity High Inc Ret Acc.

Euro Disc Ret Acc.

Euro Ethical Ret Acc.

I fold the document into quarters. I dress. New underpants, new socks. The bespoke suit, new shoes, new silk tie, new shirt. Edward bought these. The shirt contained pins. I stand on the white tiles and look at myself in the mirror. This is my reflection. I unfold the document, read.

Insight Inv Japan Eq Pf A Acc.

Insight Inv Monthly Inc Bd A Acc.

Insight Inv Monthly Inc Bd A Inc.

Insight Inv UK Discretionary A Acc.

Insight Inv UK Eq Inc Port A Acc.

In the mirror, a businessman reads a business document.

Riddle me this, riddle me that.

I may be made of wool, but I can still claw you to death and peck your eyes out.

Who am I?

# 59

Today is the day to treat yourself. Baby Girl says this. Today is the day to eat chocolate.

Owl looks sceptical.

Patsy looks at Owl.

Baby Girl asks if we will go to the newsagent with her.

Patsy shakes her head. It is Patsy's bath time. In the bathroom, Patsy rinses out the bath, puts the plug in, turns the taps. From the hall, I watch Patsy do this.

Later, Edward will take Baby Girl to dinner. Romance. Candlelit dinner for two. Edward wants us to watch. This makes it more real.

Today is the day to do things you would not normally do.

Baby Girl opens the front door. Turns, looks at me. 'Are you coming?'

Yes.

I kiss Patsy. I lift her hair and kiss the back of her neck.

Patsy straightens her back, stands. Patsy sits on the side of the bath, looks at her knees, her petticoats, the layers.

Whenever Patsy takes a bath, there are always a lot of bubbles.

I follow Baby Girl into the street.

The sky is all around us. It is that sort of day. Even in the city, surrounded by tall office blocks, the sky is all around us.

We see a tramp. The tramp wears an orange coat. The tramp has a broken leg. A car pulls away from the kerb. The tramp hears the sound of car tyres, turns, looks.

We cross the road.

Baby Girl does not want to talk about tonight. I ask Baby Girl what she will wear and she tells me that she does not want to tell me.

In the newsagent, Baby Girl looks at the chocolate bars, the wrappers. Baby chooses chocolate. Picks up a bar of chocolate. Another, another.

A man pushes past.

Edward and Baby Girl will spend the night together in a hotel. Edward wants us to watch. This makes it more real. No. It will make it less real. You watch television. Television is not real. Do not tell Edward this.

Baby Girl chooses four bars of chocolate.

The newsagent counts the change into Baby Girl's hand. Baby looks at the change. Her mouth moves as she counts. The change is correct.

Outside, Baby holds the bag open, looks inside.

There, inside.

Baby will eat one of the chocolate bars. Baby's fingers tear the wrapper. I take half. I hold the chocolate-coated biscuit with my fingers. Even in this weather, the chocolate melts.

Take pictures, Edward said. I have a digital camera.

We walk back slowly. We eat the chocolate.

Tonight, Baby will do something she has never done before. Baby is excited, nervous.

Edward showed me the digital camera. This happened yesterday.

Do you know how to work it?

Yes.

Do you know how to zoom in, out?

Yes.

I noted the name of the camera, the type of memory card the camera contained. This, in my head.

When we arrive at the flat, the carrier bag is empty. Chocolate on our mouths, fingers. Owl would not approve. Yet Owl will happily bathe in vole blood.

# 60

Is this the point? Or, is this beside the point?

I look at myself in the mirror. I stand on the white tiles and gaze at my reflection.

I will walk out into the bar and ask Edward for a job.

Edward, I am good with computers.

Edward, I am a people person.

Edward, I look the part.

Bespoke suit, new shoes, new silk tie, new white shirt.

The mirror is huge. The mirror covers the wall. Cut into the mirror, three round holes. In each hole, a sink, taps.

Edward, I can send email, I can install software, I can defragment a hard drive. I await your response.

Edward, I am an invader.

I open the mirrored door, look out into the bar. Edward has not arrived.

I close the door, wash my face, wet my hair. I run my fingers through my hair. Patsy ran her fingers through my hair. This happened last night. Patsy told me that I must help her, that something must be done. I wet my hair and think about this.

I open the door. Edward has arrived. I watch Edward cross the room to the bar. I will join him. Edward, I have something to tell you. Edward, I need to ask a favour.

When I reach the bar, Edward is sitting on a stool.

Hello, Edward.

Edward looks at me, smiles. 'How are you, Michael?'

I tell Edward that I am fine. But, I am not fine. I do not tell Edward this.

'You look smart, Michael.'

Yes.

Edward asks the barman for a bottle of lager. The barman opens a fridge, takes out a bottle, removes the cap, places the bottle on the bar. The barman pours the lager into a glass.

'Do you understand what is expected of you this evening?'

Yes.

'You watch. You don't interfere. You do not touch. Did you bring the camera?'

I tap the side pocket of my jacket. The camera is thin. The camera fits into my pocket.

'Show me.'

I take the camera from my pocket.

'Return it to your pocket. Sit.'

I sit on the stool beside Edward's stool. I invade the stool.

'This lager is Japanese. Shall I get you one?'

I look at the glass of lager, the empty bottle.

Edward asks the barman for another bottle of lager.

Edward looks at his watch. 'Dinner is at nine thirty. Then we go to the hotel.'

I nod.

'Were you at the flat today with Baby?'

Yes.

'Did she get ready? Did she find the dress I left out?'

Baby Girl did find the dress. I tell Edward this. Edward left the dress on the bed. The dress is pretty. The dress is evening wear. Baby showered, washed her hair. Baby Girl applied make-up. I watched her do this. When the dress was on the bed, I touched it. Fingers invade the material. Baby put on her green tights, her black shoes. Baby Girl put on the dress.

Edward looks at me. 'You're very quiet this evening, Michael. Even for you. Is there something wrong?'

Yes.

I want a job. I want this to be part of the deal. I tell Edward this.

Edward laughs. 'You're getting the flat. That's a pretty good deal, don't you think?'

Yes.

I drink the lager. The glass is half empty.

Behind the bar, a mirror. In front of the mirror, a row of bottles. Behind the bottles, reflections. Inside the bottles, liquid.

'I did get you a job. You quit on the first day. You didn't even quit, you just walked out.'

The job was in the post room. I tell Edward that I want to work in an office.

'You don't have the skills. If I got you a job it would be in IT. You want to work in the financial circuit, which is not possible.'

I look at my face. This, in the mirror, reflected.

'You don't want to work in IT, Michael. You want to be me. But you can't.' Edward stabs the bar with his finger. 'There are things that I have which you cannot have. That is

the point that I intend to make tonight. I want you to understand this.'

But Edward.

There are things that you have that you cannot have.

I want you to understand this.

I do not say this.

# 61

The taxi stops outside the restaurant. Edward steps onto the pavement. I step onto the pavement. The taxi drives off.

In the back window, the sky, reflected, black.

Edward paid the driver using his credit card. Edward returns the card to his wallet. The wallet is made of leather. I do not own a wallet. Edward puts the wallet into the back pocket of his trousers.

Edward looks at his watch.

'I'm nervous,' Edward tells me. 'I bet she gets cold feet. I bet she loses her nerve and doesn't come.'

In bespoke suits, we stand.

Two men walk past, not wearing suits. The men are untidy, scruffy. The men are not like Edward, me.

'I haven't slept with my wife for twenty-five years,' Edward says. I do not know why Edward tells me this. To me, the information has no value.

A dog walks past. Then, a man. The dog looks at us. Then, the man looks at us. There is humour here.

Edward watches the man and the dog, looks at me, moves his eyebrows, speaks. 'Michael, do you have sex with Patsy?'

I tell Edward that we have done it, that we do not do it.

When Patsy wants to have sex, I tell her that we have already done it. Is this true? I do not know. This is what I tell Edward.

And that is none of your business.

We wait.

With hands in bespoke trouser pockets, we wait.

We look at the reflection in the restaurant window. Us, reflected. Us, flat, with no meaning. The window is black. There are unanswered questions.

We wait.

A taxi pulls up at the kerb. The door opens. Inside, Patsy, Baby Girl.

Edward smiles. Baby Girl did not get cold feet.

Patsy in black tights, black skirt, purple duffle coat. In make-up, Patsy looks like Owl.

The pavement is broken, cracked.

Baby Girl steps up to Edward, looks at him. Edward is taller than Baby. This has meaning.

I say hello to Patsy. She looks confused. I tell Patsy that I am Michael, that we are together. I hold Patsy's hand.

Edward opens the restaurant door. Edward holds the door for Baby Girl, Patsy, me. Edward walks through the door. The door swings closed.

# 62

Two tables for two. Not a table for four. Two tables for two. Push the tables together. Two couples, side by side. Two plus two equals four. Edward holds up the fingers.

The waiter explains that the table is booked for four people.

'This is not a table for four. This,' Edward says, 'is a table for six.'

'But it is set for four.'

I look at the wallpaper. The wallpaper is a type of wallpaper called flock wallpaper. The wallpaper is as soft as Owl's tummy feathers. If only Owl were here to see it. I look at Patsy as I think this.

Edward shakes his head. 'This table is too big. Two tables for two.' Edward holds up the fingers.

'We do not have two tables for two,' the waiter says. 'It's late.'

Edward asks for one table for two, and four chairs. 'These two do not need to eat,' Edward says. The two are Patsy, me.

Patsy touches my thigh. Patsy does this whenever she feels threatened.

The waiter shows us to another table. The table is round.

Tablecloth, candle, flowers. Wicker placemats, cutlery. The waiter has brought two extra chairs.

I look at the ceiling. The ceiling is ornate. Owl would approve, if only he were here to see it. I look at Patsy as I think this.

'There isn't room for plates,' the waiter says.

Edward points at Baby, at himself. 'We two are eating. These two are not.' Edward points at Patsy, me.

The waiter is not pleased. 'I may have to speak to the manager.'

Edward says nothing. Edward has authority. The man is calm, composed. Edward puts his hands into his bespoke trouser pockets.

On Edward's fingers, rings.

The waiter walks to the back of the restaurant. Opens a door. Walks through the door. I watch the door slam. We do not hear the sound. The door is at the back of the restaurant. The sound does not reach us.

Edward looks at Patsy's bag. The bag is a purple leather sports bag. Why does Patsy have a bag? Does the bag contain Owl?

'Open the bag,' Edward says.

Patsy looks at me. Patsy does not know what to do. In black nurse shoes, Patsy is on uncertain ground.

I smile at Patsy, touch her arm, tell her to open the bag. Patsy unzips, opens the purple leather sports bag. Inside the bag, Owl.

'I told you not to bring it,' Edward says.

It?

Him.

I hold Patsy's hand and lead her outside. I explain to Patsy that Edward is delusional. We discuss Edward's deteriorating mental health. The man has lost his grip on reality.

'Edward talks out of his hat,' Patsy says.

I tell Patsy to keep the bag closed. Owl must remain concealed. It is for his own good. Tomorrow, we will take him to Hampstead Heath for a flap.

From Patsy's bag, a muffled squawk.

We walk back into the restaurant.

At the back of the restaurant, the door opens. Behind the waiter, the door slams. We do not hear the sound. The waiter weaves between tables. The waiter pulls out the chairs. 'Forgive me. Please.' The waiter gestures for us to sit.

Patsy looks at Edward, laughs.

Edward removes his jacket, hangs the jacket on the back of his chair.

I look at Edward's shirt. The shirt is white. Edward ironed the shirt. Or, Alicia ironed the shirt.

My shirt has not been ironed. Here are lines. Two across, one down. I did not iron the shirt. This is wrong. I removed the shirt from the packaging, slipped it from the clear plastic bag. Removed pins, cardboard, tissue paper. The sleeves remain creased.

We sit.

Edward reaches across the table, takes Baby's hand.

'Sit back from the table a bit.' This instruction is issued by Edward.

I move my chair back from the table. Patsy moves her chair back from the table, too. Patsy is sitting opposite me. Patsy, with that glint in her eye.

The waiter brings a bottle of water, glasses. The waiter brings menus. There are two.

Edward and Baby Girl look at the menus. The couple discuss, choose. Edward orders. Chateaubriand with mushrooms and wine jus. This for Edward. For Baby Girl, the thing with rice. Baby points with her finger.

The waiter brings wine, crusty bread.

Edward asks Baby a series of questions.

Edward makes jokes.

In Patsy's bag, Owl dreams of trees, the sky, voles. Owl gazes up at the zip. Bags look different from the inside.

Edward talks about Alicia. Baby listens, nods.

Edward does not look at Patsy, me.

Patsy is hungry. You can read this on Patsy's face.

Edward slides a plate to Patsy. Edward does not look at Patsy, just slides the plate. On the plate, crusty bread.

I stand, take some of the bread. The bread is dry. There is olive oil. I dip the bread in olive oil.

The waiter brings two meals. Edward and Baby eat.

Sweat glistens on Edward's upper lip. This is unpleasant.

Patsy laughs.

No, Patsy. Don't.

Edward waves his hand. The laugh floats away across the restaurant. Patsy's laugh lands in a man's soup.

In candlelight, Baby's eyes sparkle.

Edward asks Baby Girl if she has ever been inside a lighthouse. Baby Girl shakes her head.

'Would you like to?'

'I've never thought about it,' Baby says.

'But you are open to new experiences.'

Baby Girl smiles. 'Yes.'

'If this restaurant was at the top of a lighthouse, that would be romantic, wouldn't it.'

'Yes.'

'If a lighthouse appeared outside this restaurant tonight, would you climb the steps with me? Would you climb to the top of the lighthouse?'

Baby wriggles. 'Yes. Yes, I would.'

'We would climb to the top of the lighthouse together.'

'Yes, we would.'

'There would be the two of us, and the light, and the sea.'

Yes.

'The light would move around. Each time the light touches us, we learn something new. We learn more about each other.'

Yes. Yes. I want this.

'We discover each other up there in the lighthouse.'

Yes. Yes. I want to do this.

'The two of us.'

Yes.

Yes.

Edward, Baby Girl.

And Patsy makes three.

And Owl.

Plus one invader.

# 63

We did not speak in the taxi. Patsy did not speak. I did not speak. Owl did not squawk.

Patsy squeezed my hand.

Patsy opened the window, unzipped the zip. The breeze ruffled Owl's tummy feathers. This is undignified.

Edward did speak.

Edward told Baby Girl about his feelings for her, how it feels to touch her, how he felt the day they first met. The pain he feels when he touches Alicia.

I read signs, stickers.

Do not open the doors. This would be impractical. We would tumble out. Owl would fly up to the rooftops. Patsy's bag would fall empty.

Your skin is soft, Edward said. Your skin is pink.

Baby Girl smiled.

Baby is younger than Alicia. Baby Girl is fifteen.

The taxi driver did not speak.

There are signs, stickers. The stickers on the window are see-through. You can see the printed letters, the outline. A diagram of a window. Arrows point. The arrows indicate motion. You cannot see the sticker. There is nothing to see.

No, nothing.

And yet you look.

The taxi took us from the restaurant in East London to Bayswater, to the hotel. A black London taxi cab, room for five passengers. Edward, Baby Girl, Patsy, Owl. One other.

Patsy zipped up the bag. We climbed out of the taxi and stepped onto the pavement. My shoes, Edward's shoes.

I watch the taxi pull away from the kerb. The taxi makes a sound. The purple sports bag makes no sound. A portable nest for a bird who is going places.

The hotel is a luxury hotel. Red carpet, green foliage. Velvet curtains. Chandeliers, polished brass.

Reflected in the glass, clouds.

You cannot touch the clouds. The clouds are in the sky. You can touch the glass, the windows. Do not touch the glass. Fingers leave marks, and marks have meaning.

Clouds contain water. This is how Owl washes those hard-to-reach tail feathers. And that is the secret of Owl's beautiful sheen.

The doorman opens the door.

The doorman is as tall as the door. In his top hat, the doorman is taller than the door. To walk through the door, the doorman would duck, tip his hat.

We stand at the desk. We check in.

A room for four? Two rooms for two? A suite?

'Just us,' Edward says. Points to himself, Baby Girl. 'The honeymoon suite. These two are colleagues.' Points to Patsy, me.

The girl at the desk looks down at the desk. Feet shuffle on the tiles. The tiles are stone tiles. The walls are marble. There are pillars.

The girl at the desk asks if we have luggage. No. There is

218

Patsy's bag. The bag contains Owl. A man offers to take Patsy's bag. Patsy gives him the look Owl would give you if you touched his vintage jar of rodent liver pâté.

Third floor, the girl says.

The girl hands Edward a card. The card will open the door.

Patsy touches my elbow with her thumb. This means that something terrible will happen. We do not know what this will be. There are no further details.

Edward slips the card into his pocket.

I do not have a card. I do not control the door, the room. I am not in control. No, not yet.

Edward and Baby Girl cross the lobby to the lift area. The couple hold hands. If my hand was Edward's hand, Baby's hand would be in my hand.

I hold Patsy's hand.

At the lift, Edward presses the up button. There is a man here. Edward smiles at the man, nods. The lift doors open. The man walks into the lift. The man wears a dark green suit. We step into the lift. Edward takes Baby's hand, steps over the threshold. Edward presses the 6 button. The door closes. The man in green presses a button.

The lift moves up.

The doors, walls are mirrored. This creates the illusion of space. The ceiling is glass, with lights. The ceiling creates the illusion of open sky.

The lift lifts.

Edward straightens his tie.

The man looks at Edward's tie. The man is wearing a suit, no tie. The man takes a tie from his pocket. This tie is rolled up. The man unrolls the tie, puts it on. Edward's tie reminded the man to put on his tie. The tie is green to match the suit. The man ties the tie. I watch the man tie this.

Patsy whispers into my ear. 'Owl thinks we're flying.'

The lift stops.

# 64

Edward removes the card from his pocket. Edward swipes the card, opens the door.

Edward looks at Patsy. 'Inside this room, you do not speak. Clear?'

I tell Patsy to nod her head. Patsy nods her head.

We follow Edward into room 64.

After you.

No, after you.

The design is old fashioned, chintzy.

Shoes tread the carpet. One pair of expensive leather shoes. One pair of leather shoes. One pair of pink strappy shoes. The toes are pretty. One pair of black nurse shoes. Woolly claws remain in Patsy's bag.

Edward instructs me to close the door. I do this.

Edward draws the curtains, switches on the lamp.

Patsy slumps on the bed, drops the purple leather sports bag onto the carpet. A muffled squawk from Owl.

Edward opens a door. This door leads to the bathroom. Edward walks into the bathroom, lifts the lid of the toilet, flushes the toilet. I hear these sounds. Edward lowers the lid. Turns, returns.

I sit on the bed with Patsy.

Baby Girl is standing by the wall. Baby Girl is nervous. I can see this. Baby holds her hands behind her back.

'Come here,' Edward tells her.

Baby Girl walks towards Edward. Edward holds Baby's face, Baby's head.

I look at the carpet.

'Watch,' Edward tells me.

I watch.

I watch Edward and Baby Girl kiss.

Edward moves away from Baby Girl, steps across the carpet, to the bed, to Patsy, me. 'Michael, you have a camera. I want you to take photographs.'

I take the camera from my pocket. I press the button with my finger, wait.

'Is the flash on?'

'Yes.'

'Right. Take pictures.'

I take pictures. The camera flash lights the room. Flash, flash.

Edward instructs Baby to stand on the coffee table. Baby Girl laughs. I do not know why she does this. The wood is dark, varnished. The coffee table is ornate. Baby holds on to Edward's shoulder, steps up onto the coffee table. I do not know why Baby Girl does this.

I put the camera into my pocket. I take the camera from my pocket. There is a reason why I do this.

'Kick your shoes off.'

Baby unbuckles the straps, kicks off the shoes. The shoes fall onto the carpet.

Flash, flash.

On the varnished wood, varnished toes.

'Lift your dress. I want Patsy to see your knickers.'

Patsy does not want to see the knickers. 'I've seen them,' Patsy says.

I lead Patsy to the bathroom. To do this, I hold Patsy's hand. Behind the closed door, I explain to Patsy that we have to follow Edward's instructions.

No. We do not offer that service.

Yes, I tell Patsy. We do offer that service. We will follow Edward's instructions. Edward will give us the flat. The flat will be our flat. We will live in the City with Owl.

In bespoke woollen feathers, Owl will rule the world.

I open the bathroom door.

Baby Girl is sitting on the bed. Baby has stripped to her undies. In bra and knickers, Baby Girl reclines on the bed. In Baby's hand, Yelper.

I look at Edward.

Edward looks at me. Edward tells me to take pictures.

I photograph Baby Girl. This, as instructed.

I put the camera into my pocket. I take the camera from my pocket. There is a reason why I do this.

There is a knock at the door.

Yes?

At the door, a man. The man holds flowers, five pink bouquets. Pink is Baby Girl's favourite colour. Edward carries the flowers to the bed, to Baby.

Baby Girl laughs.

Patsy arranges the flowers on the bed. This, as instructed.

Edward kicks off his shoes.

Edward removes cufflinks, shirt, socks.

Edward drops his trousers.

Edward climbs on top of Baby Girl.

As Edward does this, Patsy shouts something, moves towards Baby Girl, opens Baby's fingers.

Edward looks up, turns.

Patsy opens the window, throws Yelper out of the window.

Yelper soaring through the air. Yelper lands among rubbish bins, brambles, drains. We do not see this. The curtains are closed.

Patsy emerges from the curtains, collects the purple leather sports bag, opens the door, walks out, slam.

I run towards the door.

'Stop,' Edward says.

I stop.

'Let her go. Take pictures.'

I do this.

This, as instructed.

This, with Patsy out in the world, in the dark, in traffic.

# 65

Edward shows me the photographs. He has had them printed. Or, Edward printed the photographs. Edward bought a photoprinter and printed the photographs.

Edward thanks me.

The pub is called the Three Bells. There are not three bells. There are no bells. I know this. Edward does not know this.

There is a lot that you do not know, Edward.

The pub is in the City, ten minutes' walk from Edward's office.

Men wear suits. This, like Edward. This, like me.

With his hands above the table, Edward moves the photographs, shows me the photographs. Look at this one. Yes, and this.

I look at the photographs.

Baby Girl, nude.

Baby Girl, held open.

Baby, Edward.

'I thought there would be more,' Edward tells me.

I take one of the photographs, open my jacket, move the photograph towards the inside pocket. This is a test.

Edward grabs my arm. 'No, Michael. I need to keep hold

of these.'

I hand the photograph to Edward.

I relax, drink.

The wood is dark brown, varnished. This pub is clean. On the wall, paintings. I look at the paintings.

I tell Edward I want a job.

'Michael, I gave you the flat. I remain the legal owner but basically it's yours.'

I thank Edward for the flat.

I tell Edward I want a job.

Edward drinks from his lager. Gulp, gulp. Adjusts cufflinks. I watch Edward do this.

I look Edward in the eye, say, 'You were right about the photographs.'

'What?'

'You said you thought there'd be more.'

Edward looks at the photographs. 'Yes. What happened to them?'

'I kept them.'

'You can't have kept them. They were all on here.' Edward takes the camera from his pocket, removes the memory card, places the camera on the table, drops the memory card onto the table.

I take a camera from my pocket, place it on the table. Edward watches me do this.

Edward looks at the cameras. There are two. The cameras look the same, are the same.

'Michael, did you have this camera with you in the hotel room?'

Yes.

Edward puts his hand on the camera. 'This camera?'

Yes.

'Both of them? These two cameras? You took pictures with both?'

Yes.

Edward sits back from the table, drops his hands to his sides. 'Michael, are you blackmailing me?'

Yes.

Edward looks at me, opens his mouth, does not speak.

Edward shakes his head.

Edward looks away.

Edward grabs the camera, opens it. 'Where's the memory card?'

I say nothing.

'Is it at the flat?'

The memory card is not at the flat.

The memory card is inside Owl.

Owl is a secret agent, a spy.

'Michael, I can't find you a job at the kick of a shoe. I can pull strings but remember you have no financial background. If I gave you a job they'd think I'd flipped my lid.'

Pull strings. Flip your lid.

Do this.

Edward is nervous. Edward stands, shakes. 'Look. I will get you a job but it won't be the job of your dreams.'

# 66

'This is the computer,' the man tells me.

I know that.

It is not a meringue.

It is not a ballet shoe.

It is a computer.

'You can sit in the corner. Plug this into the socket.'

I look at the man.

In the man's hand, a three-pin plug.

I reach under the desk, fit the plug into the socket, flick the switch, crawl backwards, stand.

I wait for the PC to boot. The man logs on to Windows 2000. The computer is slow. The screen changes colour. Icons appear, one by one, slow.

'You don't have to wear a suit, by the way.'

I look at the man. The man wears trainers, T-shirt, jeans. On the T-shirt, a cartoon face.

The man sips, stirs, sits. The soup is in a plastic cup. The soup was made by a machine.

Reflected in the screen, my bespoke suit, my face.

The man turns to a filing cabinet, opens the metal drawer, finds a pile of documents, drops the documents onto the desk. 'You're basically inputting figures. I'll highlight the column in red.' The man finds a pen, draws a line beside a column of figures. The pen is not red. The pen, the line, is blue.

Remove the cap, write it down.

I look at the numbers. The numbers have no meaning.

The man moves the mouse, clicks an icon, opens Microsoft Word. 'Just type them up in Word and I'll paste them into the spreadsheet later.'

The man walks away.

The man sits at his desk, at a PC.

I look at the door. A man walks past the door. The man wears a suit, a tie. The man carries a briefcase.

A woman walks past. The woman wears a suit.

I type figures.

54872

63242

2526

There are more like this.

I type for one hour.

I look at the door. Edward.

Edward looks at the man. Edward walks into the room, puts his mouth to my ear, says, 'Is everything all right?'

No.

I stand, walk past Edward, to the door.

'Yes. Let's get a coffee.'

No.

Pull strings. Flip your lid.

'It's not going to work,' Edward says. 'You cannot black-mail me to do something that I cannot do. I don't believe you anyway. I searched the flat. I went through your pockets.'

Edward searched for the memory card. We watched Edward do this. Edward ran out of places to look.

Edward looked inside the cereal packets, the fridge. Edward moved the bed.

Patsy laughed.

Edward shook his head.

Edward did not look inside Owl. Edward did not squeeze Owl's tummy, discover the hard angular shape.

Owl smeared the memory card with bat-blood and black-currant jam, swallowed.

I look at Edward.

'I think you gave it to Patsy, I think that's what she threw out of the window. Either that or you lost it.'

No.

Baby Girl is fifteen. You will go to prison. I tell Edward this.

I walk out of the office, to the lift.

I walk through the foyer, out through the main door, out, out into the street.

# 67

Patsy waited for me in Box, the bar opposite Edward's office, the bar where we first met Edward. Patsy saw me through the window. At Patsy's table, I told Patsy about the figures, the PC, Edward. 'I walked out,' I said.

In my pocket, the memory card. Owl coughed it up, spat it out.

'We'll go back to the flat,' I said. 'Don't forget your bag.'

Patsy picked up the purple leather sports bag. Inside the sports bag, Owl.

But, the sports bag did not contain Owl.

'He's at the flat,' I said.

When we got to the flat, Patsy could not find Owl.

I helped Patsy look for Owl.

Owl?

Where have you gone?

Owl took the tube to Hampstead Heath.

Owl popped out to stretch his wings.

Owl flew too close to the sun, scorched his wings, turned to black dust.

'He's not here,' Patsy said. 'Baby Girl must have taken him.'

We emptied the cupboards, dropped the contents onto

the floor. We lifted the bed.

'She took him because of what I did to Yelper.'

Patsy threw Yelper out of the window.

'We have to leave,' Patsy said. 'It's not safe.'

We did leave.

I bought an envelope, paper, a pen. I wrote a note. Remove the cap, write it down. The note explained to the police. I wrote Edward's name and address, and Baby's name, Rebecca. I wrote Baby's age, fifteen.

We walked to the Post Office. There was a queue. We had to wait.

I held Patsy's hand.

Edward will lose his wife, his daughter, his home. Edward will lose Baby Girl.

What I cannot have, you cannot have.

Edward will lose his job.

# 68

The garden has not changed. Clouds failed to roll. Behind the tall hedgerows, plants did not grow. On the grass, the wheelbarrow remains upturned, the wheel rocky with concrete.

The house hid from the eyes of others, us.

In the bedroom, a woman spills her tea. Dabs tea from her nightie, or tea-coloured tights.

As a child, Patsy was bigger than her mother.

'I wasn't allowed to play in the garden,' Patsy tells me. 'I played in the road.'

In Patsy's hand, the key. This, kept from childhood. Patsy's hand pushes the door.

The hall, the downstairs loo, the lounge.

The kitchen where Patsy's mother would light the hob. The gas would extinguish the match.

On the stairs, trainers. On the stairs, boots like old-fashioned kettles.

'You had to walk on the edge, on the wood.'

The bathroom where Patsy explored her body. Patsy tells me this.

Behind this door is Patsy's mother's bedroom.

Behind the door, Patsy's mother lies bedridden.

Behind the door, the woman is dead.

Patsy knocks, turns the handle. The handle is made of plastic, the colour of milky tea.

I hold Patsy's hand.

'I always get told off going in here.'

Today, Patsy will not get told off. Mouth open, teeth grave-shaped, Patsy's mother is dead.

But Patsy's mother is not in the bedroom.

On the bed, Patsy's mother's diary. Patsy opens the diary.

A woman who opened her mouth to eat, to shout.

In the back of the diary, a photograph. Patsy as a child. Patsy the length of Patsy's thigh. This Patsy could fit inside Patsy's stomach.

The owl is a nocturnal bird, Patsy's mother wrote. The owl has forward-facing eyes and ears. The owl has a beak.

'She wrote about Owl,' Patsy says. 'She hasn't even met Owl.'

The owl looks like a tree part. The owl has eyes that clench and drain.

'Owl wouldn't do that,' Patsy says.

Patsy turns the page.

Patsy turns.

Oh.

Owl.

But Owl is dead.

Owl, stuffed with garlic cloves, torn playing cards, cotton reels, pins.

Patsy puts her hands to her face, closes her eyes, cries.

I hold Patsy.

I hold Owl. I lift Owl from the dresser, hold him.

I tell Patsy to wait.

Downstairs, I cut Owl open. I remove these from Owl. Garlic cloves, torn playing cards, cotton reels, pins. These, I throw out of the window. I open drawers, cupboards. I find needle, thread. I find white polyester stuffing. I stuff Owl with white polyester stuffing. This, without anaesthetic. I stitch Owl together, sew him up. I close Owl at the tummy.

Upstairs, Owl flies into Patsy's arms.

Patsy cries.

I tell Patsy that we will always be together.

Here, with nothing, we stand in the room.

At the window, above the trees, office blocks.